We/She

edited by Cherry Potts and Katy Darby

ARACHNE PRESS

First published in UK 2018 by Arachne Press Limited
100 Grierson Road, London SE23 1NX
www.arachnepress.com
© Arachne Press 2018
ISBN:
Print: 978-1-909208-62-9
ePub: 978-1-909208-63-6
Mobi: 978-1-909208-64-3

Printed on wood-free paper in the UK by TJ International,
Padstow.

Acknowledgements

A Crowing Hen © Arike Oke first read Liars' League London *Treason & Plot* November 2012

At the Bottom of the Sea of Troubles © Lucy Ribchester first read Liars' League London *Slings & Arrows* April 2015

Bad Plates © Peng Shepherd 2018

Birth Plan © Uschi Gatward first read Liars' League London *Beginning & End* May 2014

Cages © Joanne L. M. Richards first read Liars' League London *Beauty & Beast* August 2014

Comeback Special © Katy Darby first read Liars' League London *Kings & Queens* June 2013

Desperately Seeking Hephaestion © Elizabeth Hopkinson first read Liars' League London *National Gallery Inspiration* July 2016

Destiny's Children © Rosalind Stopps first read Liars' League London *Parent & Child* July 2015

The Dead Wives' Club © Ilora Choudhury first read Liars' League London *Flesh & Bone* October 2016

Gloves © Elisabeth Simon first read Liars' League London *Clean & Dirty* February 2016

Joy © Julia Kent first read Liars' League London *Dark & Stormy* October 2014

The Lost Species © Jenny Ramsay first read Liars' League London *National Gallery Inspiration* July 2016

One Beautiful Day © Elizabeth Stott first read Liars' League London *Stage & Screen* May 2016

Smoking Ban © Jennifer Rickard first read Liars' League London *Dungeons & Dragons* July 2015

Some Carpets To Remain © Carolyn Eden first read Liars' League London *Saints & Sinners* July 2008

The Real McCoy © Cherry Potts first read Liars' League London *Weird & Wonderful* June 2014

Ugly Duchess © Fiona Salter first read Liars' League *London National Gallery Inspiration* July 2016

We/She

Contents

A Crowing Hen
Arike Oke

A whistling woman and a crowing hen can drive the Devil out of his den.
Proverb used by the Hessle Road, Hull, fishing community.

When I'd finished rubbing down the stove I took a bucket and brush out to scrub my doorstep. Mam was out there on her own step. I hadn't moved far when I'd married Freddie. 'All right Mam?' I said. I had to ask her in for a cup of tea.

'Not pregnant yet?' Mam asked. I looked at the mantel clock. It was a minute past. Seemed always to be that time.

'We're trying, Mam,' I said, the same answer as usual. 'He doesn't get much time away from sea now. He wants to get enough saved up for when we have a family.'

'The way I hear it,' Mam said, picking up a spoon, stirring her tea, 'he'll have another mouth to feed soon.'

I blinked at her. 'I'm not pregnant,' I said.

Mam examined her reflection in her spoon and said, 'There's muck on this.' She dropped the spoon back on the table. I felt the ground jolt underneath me. I bit my tongue and asked after the little ones. Mam barged on, gargling gossip. This was the third year in a row that Mam hadn't been pregnant; maybe she was finally done with all that. At nineteen it was my turn. I felt her eyes patting down my dress where it slumped empty over my hips.

*

When Freddie's boat came back from sea the house was scrubbed to shining. I brushed my hair out and drew it away from my face. I'd spent all afternoon cooking. Steak-and-kidney pie, and jam sponge for afters. The lard bought with the last of my house money. The smell drifted out of the house and down the street. The little ones came over from Mam's with big eyes. 'Got enough for us, Biddy?' they asked. I chased them off. Our brother Tommy was on the same boat so there'd be something special cooking over at theirs anyhow.

Freddie came in and slung his kitbag down on the floor like his whole body wanted to follow it. I put my hand on his cheek. It was cold, hairy, and rough, like a sea animal's skin. He rubbed his face into my hand. 'Your hands are soft,' Freddie said into my palm. My hands were rough as any woman's: made into leather by hot water and carbolic soap.

I took him to the table and sat him down. I poured him a beer and he stared at the bubbles rising in the glass. The seam across his face seemed paler than ever. His hair was so blonde it was almost white. I wanted to feel the heat of him. I'd been cold so long while he was away.

After a while Freddie said, 'Okay girl.' He lifted me off his lap and reached for his boots.

'You're off out.' My voice fell, flat, onto the floor at his feet. A pause stretched between us.

'Bridget –'

'Just stay in with me, can't you?' I tried to put my arms around him but he pushed me off. I could feel the restless sea moving in him.

He didn't come back until late next morning. His clothes were wet. Mam told me later that he'd been found sleeping outside the pub. They'd had to put a bucket of water over him to wake him.

He only got three nights at home between sailings. He hadn't spent a single one at home. I ironed his clothes and laid them out on a chair-back. He dressed without looking at me. He greased his hair and went to call for Tommy, his best mate, my big brother.

The night I met Freddie, two autumns ago, Tommy peacocked around the kitchen in the clothes Mam had just ironed. The little ones were impressed with the bits Tommy brought for them. For me he brought stories of the sea. He talked about the pancakes of ice that could rip out the hull of a boat. He told me about the harshness of his skipper and how the cook himself had been put on a bread-and-water diet, after threatening to go on strike. 'He's from the East,' Tommy had told me, like I knew what that meant. He showed me where the salty sea-frost had cut furrows into his hands. The skin was red, raised, cracked. He took off his boots to show the fat blisters along his feet. I promised to knit him thick socks. It was all I could think of. He said, 'You're a good 'un.'

That night there was no sign that Tommy's feet hurt as he strutted around the kitchen. Dad was still at sea; for a few days Tommy was the man of the house. Tommy's floor show was interrupted by a rattling at the door.

'Freddie,' Tommy greeted the stranger at our door.

'You owe me a drink, you'd better have your money ready,' the stranger said. His words were croaky. His nose was bent oddly so instead of being straight like Tommy's, it listed to one side. Tommy shouldered past me, brushing off his clothes, and was gone with the stranger. Like two river creatures flickering and vanishing in dark water, they were there and then they'd gone.

Tommy's second day between sailings was spent in bed, and in the evening Freddie came to pick him up again. Tommy was still in bed when Freddie turned up, thudding not knocking at the door. Freddie sat at the kitchen table answering Mam's questions with short creaking responses. I sat in the corner turning the heel of the sock I was knitting.

'Could you make me a pair of those?' Freddie said. He had to repeat himself; I didn't understand him the first time. Mam threw a fork at me.

'Don't be ignorant, girl,' she said.

'I can knit you socks if you need them,' Mam said to Freddie. 'Where's your mam or sweetheart though?'

'My family's in Noreg,' Freddie said, slowly, looking at me. 'I'm from Norway. I'd like it if you could find the time, Bridget. Tommy told me your name. I don't have anyone here to do that for me. I'm in lodgings.'

Everyone around here had brown eyes except for me and Freddie. His eyes were blue, like the sea, or the sky. No, more like the sea. I couldn't see into them. I lost pieces of language when I looked at those eyes. I couldn't reply, though I felt Mam's fury building. Tommy came down the stairs then and the men flickered out, shining in their onshore threads.

Between the second day and the third day I didn't sleep. By the time Tommy was packing his kitbag I had two sets of socks made.

'Can you give Freddie this pair?' I asked Tommy. 'They might not be any good, I'm sorry.' I put the socks on the table.

Tommy picked them up. He pulled the ribbing between his hands and rubbed the grain of the stitches with his thumb. 'They're grand, Bridget, thanks.' Then he was gone again. He didn't look back, because if you look back you won't come back. I never said 'Goodbye', because if you tell a fisherman that, you'll never see him again.

*

When the birds were bringing in the dawn with groggy chirping I heard the shuffle of the front door as it opened and closed. I wasn't asleep. I closed my eyes when Freddie entered our room. I felt his warmth near to me, smelt the sourness of his breath. His stiff chin-hair scratched when he kissed my forehead. I kept my eyes closed.

Freddie lay down beside me. I could tell from his stillness that he wasn't asleep. A scent I didn't recognise seeped through Freddie's smell. Something womanly. He turned his body to me and moved his hand inside my nightdress. He handled me until

I was face-down and underneath him. My nose filled with the scent of soap, rising from my laundered sheets.

I couldn't hear the birds outside any more. Seemed to me that this time, before it's decent to get up, is when bad thoughts become real. He couldn't be seeing another woman. That couldn't be what I smelt on him.

I made eggs and bacon while he packed his kitbag. It's our sailing-day tradition. I put new socks out for him, thick red hand-knitted socks. He folded them slowly and put them in the top of his bag. When he left he held the back of my head; stroking my hair, he pulled me towards him and kissed the same spot he'd kissed when I pretended to be asleep. He emptied the loose change from his pocket onto the table, to avoid bad luck at sea. Then he was gone, no goodbyes, not on sailing-day, not unless you never want to see your man again.

I sat at the table, rolling the coins around in my fists. Then I went back to bed. Lying on top of the bedclothes I said out loud, 'He's not seeing no-one else. He's mine.' I kept repeating this, rolling the words around. I don't remember falling asleep, I swear. I didn't mean to dream it.

*

In the dream I'm walking to the docks through streets of dark-windowed terraces. My vision telescopes down to a focused circle: the docks are all I can see. I can hear the river rolling through the town. The river is all I can hear. My footsteps, breath and heartbeat become muted.

I step onto the docks. The sound breaks. I can hear everything now. It's a clamour: men's voices and money clanging onto the stone. Boys laughing and yelling as they scramble for the coins. It's all a tumble and a mess of people. I have been to the docks once before in my waking life, and nothing has changed.

There he is: Freddie. His head is up, scanning the docks for his boat. He is true to taboo and doesn't look back. Goodbye, say my thoughts before my lips echo them. I feel a snake uncoil in

13

my chest and then re-spool around my heart, squeezing tighter.

'Freddie,' I whisper. He turns around, sees no-one, turns back. He boards the ship.

'Freddie,' I say. The word leaves my throat raw.

'Freddie,' I shout; the word is gunshot in my ears. I am deafening myself.

Freddie turns, despite tradition, and scans the dockside. I see his face change when he finally spots me. The colour leaves his face. I lift up my arm. It's as heavy as an anchor chain. I wave at him with difficulty. 'Goodbye,' I say. With one word I break tradition and something is unleashed.

If he loves me, if he's true to me, then the bad luck won't touch him.

*

I woke up shivering; my whole body shuddering and shaking. I pulled the wool blanket that Freddie bought up to my nose. 'It was only a dream,' I whispered.

Winter was riding in and sunlight receded more each day. I put the dream out of my mind. It wasn't real. I kept myself awake at night cleaning and re-cleaning. Knitting baby things, pulling them apart and re-knitting them. The night before Freddie's boat was due back, sleep took me while I was sitting on a hard chair in the kitchen desperately sorting buttons.

*

In the dream Freddie is home. He is playing with a young girl. The girl has my hair, long and dark. I know, somehow, that I've plaited it for her. I've never seen this girl before. They're both laughing. I join them, putting my arms around Freddie, looking into his sea-blue eyes. He says, 'I love you.'

I smile and reach out an arm to include the girl. The knowledge unfurls: she's our daughter. She comes into the circle of the hug. I look down and see that her eyes are green, same as mine. She's crying.

I taste salt.

I woke up lolled over the kitchen table. Someone was at the door. It was Mam, carrying a packet of biscuits. She told me the news as I put the kettle on the stove. There'd been a storm at sea. All hands lost. Freddie wasn't coming back.

I suppose Mam was waiting to see how I'd react. She crackled the biscuits inside their plastic. The kettle began whistling. I felt something slide around inside my body, above my navel.

'I know,' I said. 'I already know.'

Birth Plan
Uschi Gatward

Birth partner:	husband only. No-one else to be admitted until post-natal ward.
Midwives:	would prefer female midwives and other medical staff.
Positions for labour:	would prefer active labour if possible to enable me to work with gravity.
Monitoring:	where monitoring is necessary we would like explanations as to why it is being done.
Pain relief:	gas and air. Epidural if necessary (but so that legs still mobile). Would like epidural to start to wear off before the second stage so that I can push the baby out myself.
Episiotomy:	would like to avoid if possible.
Placenta:	happy to have the injection to speed delivery and prevent bleeding.
Vitamin K:	happy for the baby to have this injection.
Visitors:	I wish to see no-one except invited guests and medical staff – no non-essential staff, sales reps, or other visitors please.

Particularly not my mother-in-law.

Actually, the same goes for my father-in-law. And my mother. We'll see them when we're ready. If they ring up to ask which ward I'm on, please tell them nothing. If they want to make the trip down to London to stay, that's up to them. We don't plan to have any visitors at home for the first week at least.

If I have to have a caesarean then my husband will fetch more clothes for me from home. He will have done the laundry while I am in hospital. He will also have stocked up on groceries (including baby toiletries in the event that the baby is premature and we have not had time to get these in). He will also, ideally long before the birth, have assembled the new chest of drawers for the baby's things. He will go out and buy a car seat so that we can bring the baby home from the hospital. He will have mopped the floors.

He will have painted the hallway, including the woodwork, so that we are not ashamed to open the door. It is fine saying that the rooms we live in are the important things, but the postman, neighbours and other people who come to the door only see the disgusting hallway, and gain a false impression of the flat.

If the baby needs medical attention, then my husband is to remain with the baby at all times. Similarly if I need a general anaesthetic for any reason then my husband should take the baby and stay with it. I would like to breastfeed, so if I am still unconscious after the baby is born then the baby should be placed on my breast to encourage it to suckle.

Please monitor my blood pressure hourly as there is a history of problems in the family.

In the event of my death, my sister has all my bank account, pension and life assurance details.

Did I mention that I particularly do not wish to see any sales reps after the birth?

Please keep my wedding dress for my baby to have when she is older. In the event of my death, that is. The shoes and veil and tiara as well.

There are casseroles and a lasagne in the freezer. Also flapjacks – I have not tried freezing these before but I am assured they will be fine.

Some of my eggs (as in ova) have been frozen too, so there is the potential for a sibling for my child. I sanction this.

The life assurance payout could be used as a deposit on a house. I believe there would also be some death benefits due from my employer – you could check this.

I am happy with an open casket and a wake as per family tradition, but please check my family's wishes.

On no account is my mother-in-law to choose hymns or readings for my funeral, nor to read at it. I have still not forgiven her for the wedding.

If you need someone to make a decision and cannot get any sense out of my husband, please try my sister.

I would like the baby to take my husband's family name.

I am happy for it to be baptised.

If the baby is baptised then my sister is to be a godparent.

I think I would like it to have a name from our list, but see what it looks like once it is born.

The baby is to be placed on its back to sleep.

My husband will need some help to look after it. I am happy for family members to contribute, but would prefer the involvement to some extent of a trained professional.

The sling, cotton wool balls and other bits and pieces are in the large Ikea bag at the back of the wardrobe.

I will leave to my husband the decision as to whether to use reusable nappies or disposables.

Please keep my grandmother's locket, my rings and other heirlooms for the baby (my sister can tell you which). My friends Marie and Katy can have some of my other pieces of jewellery if they would like them.

My sister might like my grandmother's pink bowls.

I don't know what you will do with my clothes and shoes. I hope you don't throw all of them away.

The gold cross belongs to my mother – give it back to her. She gave it to me and I love it but I've never worn it.

I need a haircut. Perhaps my usual hairdresser could do it. If he is squeamish, please work from a picture.

*

Don't bury me in my maternity clothes.

*

Please try to keep the laundry under control. Also the kitchen. If you do nothing else, try to keep the kitchen, bathroom and toilet clean. Be vigilant about mopping the floors, especially when the baby starts to crawl.

Don't leave her with the neighbours, however nice they seem. My mother can come over if you are stuck. Or I would prefer that you took her to stay with your parents, even. But they are not to take her to that evangelical church. And give all our parents clear instructions e.g. about sleeping on the back, as things have changed.

Never allow the baby to eat melon or butternut squash at your parents' house: I have seen what they do to it. If you need to prepare food for her while there, refrain from using their tea towels. This might be the time to educate your father on the subject of hand hygiene. And lavatory hygiene, for that matter.

Do not allow your mother to dress our daughter. If she buys clothes for her, ever – and you must discourage this – please ensure that they are not in that hideous shade of terracotta that does nothing for anybody. You might tell your mother that she herself would take ten years off if only she would wear normal-coloured neutrals and stop shopping at Per Una. I never did find a nice way to say it.

Keep the bathroom cupboard closed at all times because of the asbestos. Don't keep anything in this cupboard. Treat it as if it were sealed up. In fact, having it sealed up would not be a bad idea. Consult my uncle on this.

*

There is a DVD of instructions with the pram, telling you how to assemble and collapse it.

You know I would prefer it if you continued to wash the tea towels at 95°.

If you do use reusable nappies, buy a sanitising product from the supermarket to pre-soak them (you can also use this in the washing machine to be doubly safe).

There's no need to buy those expensive jars of baby food – they are full of sugar anyway. Just mash up some fruit (but not strawberries until she is a year old) or some cooked veg. Don't add salt to the cooking. Get someone to show you.

Once she is old enough for family meals, do cook a proper dinner most evenings.

*

Ruth is probably right when she says we need net curtains or blinds for safety.

Don't drink alone in the house with the baby. One beer is OK.

Don't let anyone smoke in the house, of course.

*

Before our child begins to talk, please try to break the habit of using the reflexive pronoun willy nilly.

(While we are on the subject, it is 'Excuse me', not ''Scuse, please'. 'Scusi' would be just about acceptable were you Italian, but you are not.)

*

The Christmas card list is in the bottom desk drawer, along with miscellaneous cards for emergencies. It's just family, distant family and old friends we don't see much. I tend not to bother sending to our normal circle as we see them all anyway. There's no need to keep sending to my old friends once I'm gone of course, but you could use this list as the basis for writing to people to let them know of my death and the baby's birth. Remember the non-Christians too – they're not on the list.

Should Gabriella, my former tutor, attempt to write an obituary for me in one of those 'Other Lives' slots, you are to repudiate it immediately. She has form for this kind of thing and is as cunning as a fox.

Do get the leak in the cistern sorted out sooner rather than later – we don't know what it's doing to the electrics, and I'm sure it's responsible for the damp wood smell.

If you can get the floors painted that would be wonderful, but make sure you get the baby out of the house while you do it and until the paint has fully dried.

When you bathe her, the water needs to be body temperature or slightly cooler. You could buy a thermometer if it's easier.

You know I don't believe in an afterlife, I just believe that the world goes on after me. So I don't believe I'll be watching you, but I want you to be happy.

Take her to see the flowers in the park and in the market.

People will always ask you about me, especially as the baby grows up and you collect her from nursery or from school. The baby will ask about me too, once she realises. I wonder how long it takes a child to be conscious of a missing parent?

The two of you will have a wonderful relationship. You'll have to get my mother or Katy to help with things like clothes.

If anything at all happens to the baby you must love it just as much.

I don't believe in an afterlife but I believe that we will all sleep one day. We won't be conscious of being together, but we will be.

*

Sunday morning, I can see the two of you walking along Columbia Road, past the hospice, to the flower market.

You're wearing a pink coat with flowers on the pockets. The stallholders pick you up to get a better look.

I wonder who you'll be? Who you'll look like, sound like, smell like? Whether you'll have my hair. What you'll do to the world.

Will you do this, too, one day? Will a black line spread along your belly? Will you live to tell the tale?

You're a big, fleshy egg. I'm the spoon. Carefully carrying you to the end of the race. Not trying to win, just to finish.

Don't break, don't break.

Gloves
Elisabeth Simon

Simon looked at the range of rubber gloves in front of him. They took up a whole shelf in Sainsbury's, stretching from basic single use gloves that looked faintly medical, to bewilderingly fancy gloves, hot pink with feather trims and glittering diamanté edging.

What does Alisha like, he pondered. He could picture her standing by the sink, elbow deep in the soapy water. Yes, when she twisted round and picked up the next item he was sure she was wearing gloves. Yellow gloves? He grabbed a couple of pairs of the bright yellow type and put them in his basket.

Alisha was disappointed with the state of his flat. Whenever she came over she'd end up doing the washing up, or running the vac over the lounge, or sorting out the piles of dirty laundry. He never helped. He meant to, but somehow it never worked out that he did.

Simon found that he was just staring blankly at the wall of cleaners in front of him. *Oh god, how can there be a whole frigging aisle just for cleaning products?!* He normally bought anything cleaning related from the pound shop. The bottles would then sit under the sink, untouched for months until Alisha needed them. She'd always cringe slightly when she picked them up.

She deserved better. He'd woken up that morning curled up to her soft body, so perfect in his tired and worn bed linen. He'd looked at her beautiful face, fresh against the unfresh pillow, and known that he had to make her happy. Get a decent present this year. No more cheap bottles she hated to touch. He'd thrown them all away before sneaking out this morning.

He picked up a random bottle. Flash. Perfect for kitchens

apparently. Next to it, a Sainsbury's own brand. One pound cheaper. *Nice. Wait. No. No. Only the best for Alisha.* He nodded to himself and picked up the Flash and placed it in his basket next to the Marigolds. Done. He threw in a new set of sponges as well, dithering slightly over whether to get the ones with the integrated scourer or not.

Next came the bathroom cleaners. One proclaimed its power against 'Mould and mildew'. Another was for 'Shine and Sparkle'. These both sounded good to Simon. Alisha would surely like both as well. He grabbed a bottle of each.

Then there was some bleach for toilets and some bleach for kitchens. This was a confusing new world where bleach changed depending on the room function. Again, one of each type went in the basket.

Next, some stuff that foamed, good for ingrained dirt supposedly. Dusters with a fresh lemony scent. He tested some air fresheners, and picked the one that made him gag the least. He was on a roll. No expense spared for his girl.

He took his now bulging basket to the till. Alisha was going to love this! It was going to be the best Valentine's Day present ever!

He crept back into the flat, and peeked in the bedroom. Alisha was still there sleeping peacefully away, looking as amazing as ever. She was an exceptionally heavy sleeper, making cute little snuffling noises as she slept, not that she'd ever admit it.

Simon looked at his watch. It was still only eight. He pulled the door shut, leaving Alisha to her dreams.

*

Alisha woke, and stretched lazily. The room was bright, and the bed was empty beside her. She leant over to the alarm clock; it was mid-afternoon. Strange for Simon to let her sleep in so long. Normally he'd be whining about his lunch by now. But the heavy bedroom door was shut. Maybe this lie-in was his present to her; she'd certainly had worse ones before.

Time to face the day. She rolled out of bed, careful to put her feet in the slippers rather than let them touch the carpet.

She stepped into the hall, and nearly fell over. The carpet, normally so weirdly sticky, was soft and plush to walk on. It was even a deep red, rather than the normal greyish tinge. She bent and ran her hand through the tufts – it came back clean. She looked up, the cobwebs were gone, the pictures were hanging straight. What had happened?

She walked down the stairs, noting that they too were clean. No papers littering the steps. No abandoned coffee mugs.

The lounge was also spotless. The plates of old food – gone. The random assortment of socks – gone. Even the wooden coffee table softly gleamed.

Alisha moved into the kitchen, to find Simon stripped just to his boxers and a pair of Marigolds, scrubbing away inside the oven.

'Simon?'

Simon looked up at her, his face tired but proud. 'Happy Valentine's Day love,' he said, beaming at her.

She smiled.

'Come back to bed sweetie. And bring an extra pair of those gloves.'

The Lost Species
Jenny Ramsay

I'm walking behind you – walking, stumbling – trying to fix my eyes on the triangle of sweat that clamps your t-shirt to your back. Now I'm cursing your khaki camouflage as you slip in and out of my vision, swallowed up by a tangle of lianas, palms and ferns.

'Hurry up!' you shout, without looking back. 'It's getting dark already.'

I'm going as fast as I can, hacking at the mass of vegetation that clings to my legs. You're doing the hard work – clearing the path ahead, slashing a way through the woody vines – but whatever your machete hits seems to spring back behind you with renewed vigour.

'We'll be okay,' I say, 'as long as we follow the river.'

But you're too far ahead already, my words lost to the forest.

The glimpses of your back – and your sweat-matted hair – are fewer now. Then none. I follow the trail of severed vines, but it's getting hard to see in the dimming light. I reach for my rucksack, praying that I packed my torch, though I never expected to need it. I find insect repellent, camera, snacks, water, notepad, maps. No torch.

Suddenly there's a stinging pain in my leg. I look down – ants, thousands of them, teeming and swarming over my boots. I jump away, but it's too late. They're inside my trouser legs. I yank off my boots, roll up my trousers, frantically brushing them off. The pain is intense, but I have to keep moving. There are worse dangers, alone in the jungle at night – much worse dangers than ants.

When I crash into something big and solid, I think it's a tree. Then the tree moves.

'Shh,' it whispers, 'don't move.'

It's you.

'Can you see it?' your voice is trembling, fear or excitement I can't tell.

I peer at the trees around us – I can only see a few feet in the greying light. Nothing.

You very slowly raise your finger.

Then I see it. It's there, standing wary among the trees. A dark shape. A pair of amber eyes lock with mine. Just for a moment – an instant – then it's gone.

You move fast, grabbing your torch from your rucksack. You swing it around. Shadows seem to move and slide in the torchlight. But it's gone – the creature. It's gone.

I grasp your arm. 'Was that – was that what I think it was?'

'Yes,' you say. 'Yes, yes, yes!' Suddenly you're gripping my arms, dancing me round in a circle.

'But it can't be,' I say. 'I mean it's ... you know it's...'

'It's been extinct for like a hundred years! Yeah, yeah! Except it's not – and we found it. We found it! It's the discovery of the century.'

You go quiet now, standing there in the gathering darkness. I think I can hear your heartbeat. Maybe you forgive me now for slowing us down, for keeping us out here in the dusk. I think you do, because we walk together now, your torch lighting each step; the swish of your machete slower, calmer now.

When we finally see the camp ahead, we walk much closer than usual, almost touching arms. We don't speak. We're both listening to the night, breathing it in, as though this is our last night on Earth.

We *discovered it.*

'What else is undiscovered?' you whisper into the darkness from your sleeping bag.

I almost say, 'Every new moment is undiscovered.'

But I keep quiet. Let the mystery cling a little longer to the fabric of the tent.

When I close my eyes I see you. Not your whole face at once, but parts of it – your brown eyes, your slightly arched nose, your lips pursed in concentration, a trickle of sweat down the nape of your neck. As I slip into sleep, your face starts to shift and transform – your eyes become amber, your whiskers twitch, damp black nose sniffing the air. I reach out a hand to stroke your golden fur, but you melt away into the darkness.

When I wake your sleeping bag is empty. Outside, in the pink morning light, you are peering into the small silver suitcase that you lugged for days through the jungle. There are six camera traps in the suitcase. You are opening them, putting in new batteries.

'We need to put these up again,' you say, without looking at me.

I touch your arm, 'We can't. We've got to leave today. We've only got supplies for another...'

'Don't be such a wuss,' you hiss. 'We need proof. No-one will believe us without proof.'

You persuade me, as always. We can eke out the supplies for an extra day or two. We'll eat less, rest more. You are elated when I agree. You even hug me, your tanned arms squeezing me tight against your ribs. My nose squashed against your chest, breathing in your sweat. I want to stay there forever, but you let go abruptly and turn back to the suitcase.

We work together, tying the camera traps to trees, angling the lasers, marking each route with red plastic ribbons so we can find them again. As we place the last camera, your fingers brush against mine. I look up to meet your eye, but you are looking away, through the trees, your brow furrowed in concentration.

On the walk back you are silent.

'We make a good team,' I say, smiling. But you say nothing. Your eyes are scanning ahead, searching among the trees.

Back at camp you are restless. I think hunger is making you jumpy so I give you some of my crackers. You eat all three at once. I go to wash myself in the river – it's been a long sticky day – but when I come back you have gone. You don't return till nightfall, slipping into the tent without a word, lying down in the same sweaty t-shirt you've been wearing for days. I pretend to be sleeping.

You're up before dawn of course, yanking on your boots.

'Have some breakfast first,' I call out the tent door, but you're striding off with your rucksack slung over your shoulder. I scramble to get dressed.

I don't know which camera trap you'll go to first. I take a guess, but I'm wrong – the camera's there, but not you. When you find me untying it, you're angry.

'Don't touch it!' you scream. 'You might break it.'

I stand back; let you untie it, though your hands are trembling more than mine.

Back at camp we stare at the laptop – image after image slides into view. You whizz through them quickly – a family of peccaries, a little blue bird, an agouti nibbling nuts, even an ocelot, but none of this excites you. You curse each one for wasting the shots. You start again at the beginning, scrutinising each image, examining every background tree, every leaf, every shadow. Nothing. Our creature is not there.

'We need another night,' you say.

'No. Absolutely no.'

'Just give me two more days. Please. Just two more days to find him.'

I've never heard you plead like this before.

'You can go back, take all the food,' you say. 'Take the tent too. I'll follow you in two days, I promise.'

I shake my head, 'No. We both go back. We apply for visa extensions, we get fresh supplies, and we come back again.'

You laugh, throwing your head back. At that moment I know there is no hope.

'That could take months – and by then he might have moved on, found a new territory. Our only hope is now, to strike while the iron's hot.'

If I could drag you back through the forest I would, but you're much, much bigger than me. I pack my bags, leaving you the tent and most of the food. I might not make it on my own, alone in the jungle, but now I'm the only hope for both of us. If I wait any longer I will be too weak.

I walk for hours without stopping. As dusk descends I see shapes flitting among the trees – dark shadows darting at the corner of my eye. Eventually I curl up in a hollowed-out tree trunk, my sleeping bag wrapped tight around me. I close my eyes, but all I see is your face, the crease of your brow as you peer through the trees. I try to hold on to your features, but they start to melt – your eyes turning to amber, your golden hair thickening over your face.

I must have slept, eventually. In the morning the forest seems peaceful. Birds are singing, little tamarin monkeys chattering. The path becomes easier and after eight hours I reach the wide dirt track that leads to the nearest village.

It's five more days before I've made it to the city and got a search party together – two ex-army paramedics and a local hunter who can clear a path through the forest quicker than a bulldozer. I'd hoped for more but the government won't prioritise it. He's not lost, they say, he's chosen to stay there.

We take enough supplies to last two weeks. The paramedics try to calm me down – humans can live for weeks without food or water, they say. But as we approach the camp, they start to warn me – your friend will be alive, but starvation can make people delusional, paranoid, aggressive. They tell me they have brought a roll-up stretcher and tranquillisers – just in case.

When we reach camp there's no sign of you. I search among your clothes in the tent – you must still be wearing the same khaki t-shirt, same socks, same combat trousers. The laptop is in the tent. I lift the lid and it whirs into life. An image flashes onto the screen.

And there it is – unmistakable. Its amber eyes gazing straight into mine. I gaze back for a moment then snap the laptop shut. *You did it. You actually did it.* Here is all the proof we need. We can go home now.

But where are you?

Each day we go out in pairs, scouring the areas around the camera traps and further afield. A week passes and still there's no sign of you. At night we huddle around the campfire, flinching at shadows. I try to imagine what you would do if I had disappeared. That's when I remember the camera traps – of course, why didn't we think of that? We must re-set the camera traps.

For four days we find nothing. Then suddenly, on the fifth day you are there. The others say it's a trick of the light – just shadows and leaves – but I can see you right there, peering out from behind a tree. You're in shadow, but the shape of your head, the curve of your shoulder – I'd recognise that silhouette anywhere.

The paramedics are telling me we have to go tomorrow – that we only have enough supplies for the journey back.

'Just give me two more days,' I say. 'Please. Just two more days to find him.'

I sneak out of the tent just before dawn. I will hide until they're gone, so they cannot force me. I'm tiptoeing to the forest path, but there's a crunch behind me. A hand grips my arm.

'Don't worry, this won't hurt. We just need to get you out of here.'

I try to run, but they're holding me back. The stretcher is unrolled and the paramedic plunges a needle in my arm. Before I black out, I catch a movement in the forest – a shadow. I look up, and I swear it's you, looking back at me. Just for the briefest moment – an instant – then gone.

One Beautiful Day
Elizabeth Stott

The Salters arrive as the November evening engulfs the provincial town. They park outside the Victorian civic hall as instructed by the secretary of the local music society. The Gothic ornament of the exterior, darkly streaked by pollution, is just as the Salters expect, for they have seen many such venues in their years of touring the provinces. The brief period when their names appeared at Covent Garden still warms their hearts. At least, it warms Mr Salter's heart; he is often heard reminiscing about his *Toreador*, a part he took temporarily when the incumbent Escamillo had shingles.

What would these provincial folk know, anyway? Something from *Madama Butterfly* always goes down well, and they have costumes – much repaired – dating back to their time in grander productions. They are pleased to note that the accompanist is a respectable pianist from the nearby cathedral, but Renée Salter is not pleased that they are to be supported by a local soprano, a twenty-year-old currently studying at the London School of Music on a scholarship.

Aged twenty, Renée Salter understudied Cio-Cio-San in a major production of *Madama Butterfly*, and was widely regarded for her rich soprano voice. But her plain looks and pear-shaped silhouette did not equip her for the part of the glamorous heroine, and she had to resign herself to playing the parts of older women long before she became one herself. Maurice Salter, a man of rather blocky build, was once ruddily handsome, but is now merely ruddy. However, Maurice fails to acknowledge his faded glories in his dealings with younger women, often to his wife's public humiliation.

The dressing room is dank and dim, but it is a designated dressing room and not a janitor's cupboard or backstage toilet. Renée sits before the illuminated mirror to do her make-up. Half of the bulbs are broken and the glass is foxed. It seems an apt metaphor for the pair of them. Maurice takes a swig from his pre-performance tipple. Renée dabs concealer around her tired eyes.

They are to meet the mayor for a reception before the performance. Renée wears a once-expensive gold evening gown, cut low over her meagre bosom. The effect, with a tiara and diamanté necklace, is of an antique perfume bottle. She has mended the seams of the dress and of her husband's evening jacket more than once. She hopes the lighting will be subdued and that Maurice will not drink too much. Renée seldom partakes of more than diluted fruit juice before a performance, and eats nothing.

Renée has seen a picture of the young soprano. She is all a twenty-year-old should be; lush-skinned with long, glossy hair and a cleavage to get lost in. No doubt she can outmatch Renée in sheer lung power. But the local audience will not be capable of distinguishing Renée's technical superiority from the youngster's athletic gust. Moreover, she knows that Maurice will humiliate her again. More than once she has considered leaving him, but the future for her, alone, descending into retirement and old age, is bleaker than she cares to contemplate. But tonight she will sing Cio-Cio-san's aria *One Beautiful Day*. Cio-Cio-san, of course, was little more than a child when she married the faithless Pinkerton in the story, even younger than the young soprano.

The mayor's party is the usual blend of provincial social gamesmanship, lubricated with cheap wine and fortified by savoury nibbles served on paper plates. Maurice is soon up to his ruddy nose in alcohol and attempting to bury it in the well-exposed cleavage of the soprano. A drove of paunchy middle-aged men snuffles around her like a herd of pigs at a trough. And the silly girl seems to be enjoying the flattery.

Renée is surrounded by the polyester-frocked ladies of the assorted local musical societies and feels, in her gold dress, like a battered museum specimen of exotic butterfly accidentally placed amongst the common or garden. As usual, she eats nothing, and drinks only mineral water, forgetting the missed lunch in the misery of the gathering. Not even the elderly men of the parish try to flirt with her these days. She has passed from vague allure to vaguely invisible as she approaches sixty. With this miserable thought, she faints.

The consequence is that she is told by a retired doctor to 'have a lie down', whilst the inebriated Maurice gets to sing duets with the plush soprano young enough to be his granddaughter. In the dismal dressing room she tries to make herself comfortable on a bony chaise, and is given a cup of tea and some left over nibbles by the pearl-buttoned woman assigned as her 'minder', who readily abandons her on Renée's assurance that she will be perfectly fine. The tea is already cold, and she has no appetite for the orange furry cheese things or the miserly pretzels. She should cry, but tears elude her.

In the stage mirror her face is shadowed, but there is no hiding her age, nor indeed her plain looks. She would have gone into teaching had not Maurice convinced her that they were destined to bring opera to the provinces and that one day they would have their own television show. She realises now that he had been jealous of her accomplishment, not wanting her to outshine him, even as the plain, pear-shaped older woman. Her voice had sold the tickets.

Through the door she hears blurts of sound – Maurice's rough bassoon and the bright flute of the girl. She imagines him, in his shiny evening suit and the garish red bow-tie he had insisted upon wearing, as an eager but aged cockerel in the company of a new hen. The jabbing piano sends darts of sound through her head.

Taking her coat and evening bag, Renée slips out of the back door of the hall into the drizzle of the street. She pauses at one of the posters. The photographs they used are old. It is a long time since they had professional ones taken. The girl's picture is clearly an amateur attempt, but she looks fresh and new, whereas she and Maurice are faded and outdated. Renée sees they missed one of the 'e's in her name. She has become 'Rene', unaccented.

She finds the high street full of youngsters doing the pubs and clubs, the young women dressed skimpily, with no coats, wearing platform shoes, teetering like Geisha in geta sandals.

Renée attracts glances with her gold evening gown, which swirls out from beneath her everyday coat. Some of the men comment, but good naturedly, they are not yet drunk. One of them recognises her from the poster. The drizzle will have made her make-up run and her hair frizzy. However, just being outside that grim hall and the burden of the lacklustre evening gives her energy.

At the entrance to the pedestrianised high street is a memorial of some kind, with steps leading to a modest monument with a canopied top. She climbs to the plinth and takes a throat pastille from her bag and assesses the location. She does some vocal exercises, judging the acoustics of the place. The canopy acts to focus the sound, allowing her voice to soar over the background sounds of traffic into the confined shopping street. Raindrops catch the light like sparks, but it is surprisingly mild for a night in November. A small audience gathers as she removes her coat. Renée welcomes them. She bows. She gives them some easy ballads to warm up her vocal chords. The crowd claps in approval. Her audience grows. Renée delivers some Gilbert and Sullivan and some songs from West End musicals. Her audience claps and cheers. Renée can see their hopeful faces uplifted; full of anticipation. She moves on to Carmen's habanera, a song of the vicissitudes of love. By now, the rain has stopped. Even the background traffic noise seems muted. Her voice surrounds them all like a cocoon. They are part of the song. She flirts with them, and they respond, animated. A young man pulls a red rose from a bunch he has tucked into a supermarket carrier bag. Renée blows him a kiss. An encore is demanded. She bows, raises her finger to her lips and smiles demurely. She transforms before them from the defiant, flirtatious Carmen to the poignant Cio-Cio-san, anticipating the return of her husband in the aria *One Beautiful Day*. The audience is stunned, then bursts into applause. She is received into the arms of the crowd, who walk with her back to the Civic Hall, buying her fish and chips on the way.

By the time Maurice staggers to the dressing room, his red bow-tie crooked, his nose ruddier and shiner, his ears ringing to the shrill notes of the young soprano, Renée is sound asleep in her damp evening gown. She is clutching the broken stem of a rose and smiling.

Some Carpets To Remain
Carolyn Eden

The Butchers were an ugly couple. Although Henry Butcher was a senior civil servant with a chartered accountant wife, to Madeleine the stench of abattoirs surrounded them. Janice Butcher's enormous mouth was forever open. The more she talked the wider the cavern gaped, displaying strong canines chewing every syllable as if it were rancid gristle. Even when silent Janice's teeth tended to protrude beyond her scarlet lips with her tongue darting from cheek to cheek as though foraging for further fleshy morsels. Both the Butchers had flabby podgy fingers reminiscent of flattened pork sausages.

The Butchers had proudly itemised the wonderful improvements they had foisted upon the three hundred year old cottage that Madeleine had convinced Graham to purchase.

Linoleum had been placed over the parquet flooring.

'Couldn't be fagged with all that fiddly polishing.' Janice boomed.

Double-glazed, pivoting picture windows had replaced the leaded-light casements.

'Far more practical, my dears.' Henry had grinned.

Ancient oak beams had been smothered with practical white non drip gloss.

'You'd never believe how dark and dreary it was in here!'

At least their plans to remove the 'insect-infested thatch' had been thwarted by some local 'busy-body' threatening a preservation order.

'We would have appealed, but Brussels beckons, don't y'know, so we want the England end sewn up before November.

Of course, we're letting it go for a song considering how much we've already ploughed into the place.'

*

Mr Fairweather, tutting constantly and scrawling morosely upon his notepad had sighed as he gave Madeleine his estimate for the cottage's restoration.

'However you must understand that craftsmanship nowadays don't come cheap,' he said as he tapped the wall around the mock Yorkstone fireplace. 'D'you know, there could well be an inglenook beneath all this rubbish.'

The bills were staggering. Graham frowned constantly, muttering about overdrafts and interest rates and the need to economise, economise, economise ad infinitum. The new suite of dining furniture had to be cancelled. The Aga would have to wait a year or two and as for starting a family...

By the following spring though, the Butchers' major blasphemies had been obliterated and at long last the cottage had regained much of its charm. Sweet scented logs smouldered in the magnificently restored grate and stained oak beams held gleaming brass and copper-ware. Glaring spotlights had been replaced by subtlely shaded standard lamps and the flamboyant flock wallpaper in the hallways was no more.

One thing continued to gall Madeleine. A vast swathe of opulent purple carpet stifled the sitting room floor. Beneath it was wood yearning to be nourished with polish and cosseted with fringed rugs of autumnal hues.

*

Graham was adamant. 'Absolutely not! There's no way we can run to new carpets this year. Both our cars are going to need a mint spent on them to get through their MOTs and we can't travel to town on rugs! Unless, sweetheart, you can find magical, flying, Persian ones.'

'There's a sale at Henderson's' next month. Couldn't we just manage...?'

'We can't even *just manage* what we've already spent on this place,' Graham snarled. 'Those Butchers did us good and proper! No, I mean it, not a penny more on the cottage. Not yet, anyway.'

There was no more arguing, not with Graham in resolute mood.

The carpet's purpleness seemed to screech at her every time she entered the sitting room. In certain lights it became the dreaded maroon of her old school uniform, reminding her of those incarcerated days of Latin verbs and incomprehensible calculus. At other times she saw caked droplets of blood within its swirls and remembered the dull eyes of game birds hanging in the windows of Hoskins, 'Purveyors Of Fine Meats', the shop adjacent to the hospital where her father had spent the final month of his life.

In daylight the carpet was merely an irritant, constantly splattered with minute flecks of dust however frequently it was vacuumed. Whatever her occupation – sewing, reading or relaxing in front of the television – the carpet would claim her attention, a malicious reminder of the Butchers' influence spoiling her tranquillity.

'Oh Madeleine, what a beautiful place you have here.' Tina had gushed. 'My goodness you've done wonders in such a short time. What a charming room this is!'

'Yes, it is lovely,' Madeleine said. 'Of course the carpet's got to go. Hideous, isn't it?'

'It's okay. Almost magenta, isn't it? Superb quality. Murder to keep clean, I suppose, but nice and soft!'

It amazed her at how tactful friends could be. She knew full well that, unless she pre-empted them, the moment her visitors reached the garden gate they would turn to each other whispering, 'Sweet cottage, but what awful taste in carpets!'

It was worse the nights Graham worked late. The isolation did not worry her; she was not the sort to jump at every creak or rustle, worrying unnecessarily about intruders or evil spirits. Neither was she the suspicious type. She trusted Graham implicitly. Madeleine was basically practical; a romantic yes, but an hysteric never.

Only, some evenings, especially when she was exceptionally tired, the carpet would claim her. Her eyes would suddenly alight upon a patch of it and the purpleness would swirl at her conjuring images of formless doom. She would see those gross cheeks of Janice Butcher or the gummy leer of a hatchet-wielding Henry, his piggy eyes fixed upon a procession of doomed cattle. The visions would last for a matter of seconds until Madeleine shook her head and focused once again on the normality of the white-washed walls. Then, sensible enough to bypass the drinks trolley, she would amble into the crispness of the kitchen with its soothing quarry tiles and comforting biscuit tin.

'You're alone too much!' Her mother knew everything without ever being told. 'You should start a family – you're not getting any younger, you know!'

'I know!'

'Don't tell me you can't afford to. No one can. Everything, I take it, is all right in – er – that department?'

'Yes, mother, that so-called department is fine. We're just not ready to...'

'And you should give up smoking. That's the third since I've been here!'

But Madeleine couldn't have a baby; not yet, not here, not with the Butchers' putrid clamminess pervading her home, mocking her via the carpet.

So genteel, are we? So sensitive with a proper sense of what is right and fitting? Scrub all you like, but we can still laugh at you! Close your eyes and watch us eat our rare roast beef. See the rosy droplets of blood moistening our lips!

*

Graham's promotion had been swift and unexpected. A sudden re-alignment had occurred and everyone in his department had been moved one notch upwards.

'There's not much more *Money*, I'm afraid.' Graham had this wonderful way of speaking in capitalised italics when he was excited. 'Not actual *Cash* in hand. A better *Title* of course, darling, *Assistant Deputy Controller* – sounds *Grand* doesn't it? But it's the *Perks* that'll make all the *Difference*. A Company Car! So how about two weeks in the *Sun?*'

'Rugs for the lounge?'

'Ah! One week in the sun, then!' Graham knew when he was beaten. 'Okay, but don't go mad. I've sort have grown used to this room as it is – I know you think purple's a vulgar colour but at least it's cheerful!'

That last comment, thought Madeleine, was almost grounds for divorce, if not committal, but she let it ride. Graham had not noticed the swelling in her belly and she would not tell him until she had become at peace with her home.

Graham had his obstinate streak too. Although he was delighted about the baby, he worried about the expense.

'For goodness sake, Maddy, there's nothing basically wrong with it! You needn't ever have to see it. It can go in the guest room. Our parents will want to come to stay more now, and anyway that bed your aunt gave us is so large that no one's going to notice the colour of a bloody carpet. We can't afford to throw money away so it goes up in the back room and that's my final word on the subject!'

*

Madeleine was surprised at how difficult it was to move the double divan from the guest room to the landing despite the way Felix and Bert *–no job too small–* had huffed and puffed and grunted as they had worked. To her untrained eye, it had all seemed a ploy to bolster up their fee. She soon learnt that their struggle had been for real.

And now, for the second time in a day, both mattress and base had to be transferred to the hall. Desperation gave her both the necessary strength and determination. Her finger nails were snagged and her shoulders ached, but the floor of the little eaved room was totally cleared and she could begin.

Even after only a couple of hours, the bed's tiny wheels had left their imprint upon the freshly carpeted floor and scraps of blanket fluff had become entwined in the purple pile.

She sat cross-legged upon a sheet of newspaper – determined not to allow the carpet to brush her flesh – sipping at her mug of percolated coffee as she surveyed the room.

Yes, it was right. The time had come.

Madeleine took a box of matches and her last ever packets of cigarettes from her pocket and began to smoke. She closed her eyes as the nicotine rose to her head, producing that wonderful feeling of dizziness which is the joy of inhaling tobacco after many days' abstinence. The smell was thrilling.

As she reached the point in her cigarette when the filter began to feel just a little warmer, the point described as, *leave a long stub*, she opened her eyes and leaned forward until she was practically lying on her stomach. Wilfully, with a serene smile, she ground the glowing residue of tobacco into the very centre of the purple carpet.

A brown, crusted ring appeared around the spot where the cigarette's tip rested, withered and expired. A solitary patch of the luxurious pile had become irreparably soiled.

Retrieving the crumpled stub, Madeleine chucked it into a large glass ashtray and promptly ignited another. During the course of a long, luxuriating afternoon, she revelled in the naughtiness of chain smoking, extinguishing each cigarette upon a different area of carpet. Some were spitefully screwed in tiny, circular movements, whilst others amused her by quietly dying in their own time, creating singed sores around them. Cold coffee was spooned upon those smouldering butts eager to soil beyond their designated bounds.

As dusk approached, the rectangular area to be covered by the guest bed was pockmarked with scorched craters like the scabbed, acned faces of puberty. Small clumps of unmutilated tufts cowered in the wake of the intermittent, coarse blackened pits. The pathetic margin of unblemished carpet, orphaned and useless, held no terror.

The room stank from the fumes of cremated wool mixture but wasn't there, Madeleine wondered, also just a whiff of burning flesh? Ribs, chops, cutlets, scrag-end – smouldering in a grease-laden oven?

At last she rose from her squatting position, grinned triumphantly and flung open the casement window and, in a final petulant gesture of defiance splattered dregs of coffee grounds over the desecrated floor.

She sang a tuneless lullaby as she vacuumed and, when she stood back to admire her handiwork, felt a sense of satisfaction kindred more to that of artistic creation than of vindictive vandalism.

She slid the divan bases back into the guest-room and consigned their wheels to the dustbin but found it a bit of a struggle heaving the mattress on to its perch. Her strength might have waned had she not the determination of the nesting female.

She fetched crisp white linen from the airing cupboard, meticulously folded hospital corners, fluffed pillows and draped the giant candlewick bedspread so that it evenly skirted the bed's perimeter further camouflaging her handiwork. She latched tight the windows, sprayed sparingly with lavender air-freshener and removed the foul brimming ash tray and the empty coffee mug.

The door was clicked shut; the deed, at long last, had been done. If ever she and Graham had to move house again, then Madeleine would simply generously insist that the old guest bed, along with some carpets, would remain.

Coda

That Madeleine and Graham's daughter was born with a tiny port-wine birthmark staining her cheek was, of course, totally coincidental.

The Real McCoy
Cherry Potts

Hello, dearie, don't be shy, come all the way in. On your own are you? I know, it is a bit of a shock, isn't it? Especially after all the noise and razzmatazz outside. Not what you were expecting? Well, now don't be coy; I *know* what you were expecting.

The thing about it is, you lot, what you imagine, when you think of people like us, like me, it's – it's all about sex isn't it?

You think *mermaid*, and you think pale, slender, pretty shoulders, long floaty hair. And you might allow for green hair, or green skin even, at a pinch, and you might even have been wondering about a belly button, but you were hoping for a pert bosom, don't try to pretend you weren't.

And the fact of the matter is we aren't all pretty. Some of us look like the back end of a walrus, although you'll never find us getting exactly flabby – not with all the swimming, and frankly, if you let yourself go, a shark'll finish you off in two shakes of an electric eel.

So when I say *mermaid*, or when you see that tasty little sign outside for that matter, you are not thinking colossal great things like me with generous hips and flaky scales and big floppy tits. I saw you screwing your face up, like I wouldn't notice! Are you disappointed? Thinking about asking for your money back? If I was still in the sea I'd look better, my skin wouldn't be so dry and cracked and my hair would have a good deal more bounce... and I wouldn't have put on this much weight.

I'll tell you what though; you weren't really expecting me, a genuine mermaid, were you? You thought I'd be some girlie in a clamshell bikini and yardage of slinky blue skirt with unconvincing fins. So why are you disappointed that you got the real thing? That makes no sense at all! You should be in awe, really.

See these? These are gills. Impressive aren't they? It's only because of the nose and mouth arrangement I can breathe air – and talk to you, obviously. If I had to rely on the gills I'd be dead in – oh – half an hour? Very few of us survive without the sea. Take us away from it and we pine, dead in a fortnight mostly. Fortunately I'm tough, and I can see the positive side of a career.

Of course, I was young once, but never what you'd call pretty, or little. None of us are – your average full grown mermaid clocks in at ten feet and close on 300 pounds, that's a lot of ballast, not as much trouble to move as the elephant, but the elephant can walk on her own four feet, of course.

I need my own vehicle, complete with travel tank. It' not very big, not very comfortable but it's generally only a few hours.

Do you want to get in the tank with me sweetie? You might not want to really – the water's not been changed for a week, not since we pitched the tent last Saturday. Too much effort. I should talk to my agent about that, there's bits of popcorn and dead flies and all sorts – look – cigarette ends. You people are disgusting. The things you think to throw in the sea – and the tank – well that's worse, do you think I don't notice?

What do you mean *liberation front*? What do you think this is, *Free Willy*? I'm too old to go back to the sea.

I told you, some Orca, or a Great White would snap me up within the hour, my speed swimming days are over.

No love, you'd not be doing me any favours. I'm not what you'd call content exactly, but I meet some interesting folk, here and there, like you, for instance. And we have some great sing-alongs, me and the strong man and the fortune teller, when all the punters have gone home. She's the genuine article too, that fortune teller, when we first met, in the harbour of some little place I never knew the name of, she told me I'd see more of the world than I'd bargained for. And she was right – not that much of it's been all that attractive. We bring the attractions, the bright lights, the tall stories; no point bringing them somewhere that's got all that already, is there? So it's places like Coventry and Croydon and Catford, and Stoke and Swindon and Slough, and here – no offence. Hardly ever go near the sea of course, just fluke they found me, someone not paying attention and they took a wrong turn – several, really – ended up on the harbour wall, and nearly drove the caravan into the water. How I laughed. Had a lovely chat with the fortune teller while they were sorting it all out. Spur of the moment decision really, and, well, here I am! Ta da!

Right ho, you scuttle along now lovely, you've overstayed your five minutes a bit haven't you, and I can see someone lurking behind the tent flap. Hello! Be with you in a tick! I expect you'll be wanting some candy floss, and a cup of tea? Oh, and don't tell anyone will you, sweetie, don't spoil the surprise. That's a good lad.

Hello, poppet, come all the way in now, I don't bite. I know, it's a bit of a shock, isn't it…?

Bad Plates
Peng Shepherd

I sit on the sofa, sucking on a dried sour plum. The sun is so strong it makes me squint. I put my hand on my forehead to shade my face and spit out the seed – it hits the grass and bounces, landing close to the others. I reach in my plastic bag for another one, and the tangy, sweet powder on the outside of its rough dried skin makes my tongue tingle.

My mother sets a lamp down on the cushion next to me, and fans her neck with a hand, her face pink in the humid summer heat. 'So hot here,' she says.

'Is it as hot as China, Mom?' I ask.

She looks at me, and her hand stops fluttering. 'I don't remember,' she says, and walks back inside the house.

I finish scraping the leathery fruit from the seed with my teeth and spit again. It goes wide, and rolls into a tangle of weeds. I'm trying to get them in groups of eight, because eight is a lucky number, according to my mother. She's always trying to make us more lucky. We keep a cup of water on the table in the living room and a little plant in the kitchen to balance the flow of *qi* in the house, we never hang any laundry at night, we never sweep the floors on Chinese New Year, and every birthday we always make the special soup that has only one long noodle.

But most importantly, we have the bad plates.

Bad plates are different than our regular plates. Our regular plates are all the same, off-white coloured and round with a little lip on the edge. We wash them by hand after every meal, because my mother thinks running the dishwasher is too expensive, and keep them stacked in the kitchen cupboard above the rice cooker.

The bad plates aren't for eating on, or cooking with, or even holding leftovers. They're not for food at all. We keep them on a shelf in the garage, next to the gardening tools and spare fuel can for the car. They're all from different places, and none of them match. Some have chips or scratches, others fading designs or dulling glazes, because they're so old.

But we don't call them the bad plates because they're old or damaged or don't match.

We call them the bad plates because they're for breaking.

'Bad things always come in threes,' my mother warns me every morning on my way out the door to school, just like the first time I saw her break the bad plates. I was only five then, and one of the legs on my dinner chair had just snapped. 'That's why we smash two plates now.' She had lowered the heavy plastic bag onto the cement garage floor, lifted the hammer, and glanced sidelong at me with a smile. 'Ready?'

I covered my ears with my hands and squeezed my eyes shut as she brought the hammer down on the bag, shattering the bad plates inside.

*

My mother says of all the things we do, this is the most important.

You can do all the lucky things you can think of, like putting a crystal over the door or keeping a money tree in the house, but if a bad luck spirit finds you, you have to have a way to get rid of it, or it will just keep taking all the good luck you worked so hard to get until it gets to three. That's what the bad plates are for, to stop the curse right away. As soon as a bad thing happens – like the time my mother crashed the car into a light pole when backing up in a parking lot, or the time I fell off the fence and hurt my arm, or even the time a burglar broke into the house while we were out for the afternoon and stole our stereo – my mother goes out to the garage, takes a plastic bag out of the pile in the corner, puts two of the bad plates inside, ties it off to so the broken crockery won't fly everywhere, and then smashes the life out of it with a hammer. Then she drops the whole thing into the garbage can, brushes off her hands, and comes back inside to do whatever she was doing before.

Two broken dishes make three bad things total, and the bad luck curse is over. It always works.

*

I eat another dried sour plum and look around at everything in the front yard. Almost our whole house is out here now. The dining chairs, coffee table, and bookcase are all scattered around the driveway, with boxes full of little things at the front. My mother opens the garage door behind them and puts the TV in there, so the sun doesn't beat down on it while we wait. From where I'm sitting on the couch in the middle of the lawn, I can see the bad plates on the shelf behind the big black screen, like they're hiding in the dark. After so many years here in America, there are only two boxes left, but there are still plenty of plates, enough to last for years. I want to ask my mother why we can't just break two bad plates to stop this bad luck, why we have to sell everything instead, but she's still inside, gathering more things, so I just turn the plastic bag of plums in my pocket over and over with my fingers and keep looking out at the road. I want to ask her what 'eviction' means too, but I know it'll only upset her more, and she won't answer anyway. Her eyes have been red all week.

A few cars go by and slow down, examining everything on display. One or two even roll down their windows to get a better look, but they all keep going. I spit out a seed and eat another plum.

A pickup truck pulls up to the driveway and stops. A man opens the passenger side door and leans out without cutting the engine. 'Are you selling a refrigerator today, by any chance?' He calls out to me.

I shake my head.

'Thanks anyway!' The man waves and pulls himself back into the truck as it rolls away.

After that, no one comes by for a long time. I go through at least four more dried sour plums without seeing a car.

*

When she first came to America, my mother told me that all she brought with her were two cotton dresses and five big boxes of bad plates. She left everything else, all her other clothes and belongings, because you could only take so much, and the plates were the most important, she said. What good would clothes and belongings be if you had no way to protect them from bad luck? I asked her once why she couldn't just get more bad plates when she got here, why she had to carry those heavy boxes all the way across the ocean, but she just smiled and clucked her tongue at me. 'They are special, Jiayi,' she answered. 'They come all the way from China.' She tapped me on the nose like she always does when she is telling me something about her old home. 'Someday when you grow up, and you go visit yourself, you will understand.'

It took her ten years to collect them all, and ten more to make them strong enough to fight off the bad luck. She had to pray to our ancestors and put the plates by the graves overnight with an offering, asking for their help. Then the next morning she would go to the graves again and sweep the headstones and clean the weeds away, burn the incense sticks, and leave more fresh offerings for them to say thank you. She says our ancestors are very powerful, that they were very rich and very lucky a long time ago. 'I named you after your great-great-great-great-grandmother,' she told me on my eighth birthday, the luckiest birthday. 'She was very lucky, so you will be lucky, too.' She never explained why my great-great-great-great-grandmother was so lucky though. Or why we aren't anymore.

*

'Jiayi, go do your homework,' my mother is back again, squinting down at me under the sun, holding a case of vinyl records under one arm and a flower vase under the other.

'I like the records,' I say. 'Do we have to get rid of those?'

'I told you. We need money or we can't buy groceries.' She turns away from me and sets the records and vase down on one of the little end tables. 'You want to eat, don't you?'

I look down at my plastic bag of dried sour plums. There are only two left. I tie the bag off and put it in my pocket, for later. 'I just like the records though. Can't we keep the records?'

'Jiayi, stop it,' my mother snaps. For a minute, she looks like she's going to cry, or smack me on the cheek, but then we hear a car.

'Hello, welcome,' my mother turns from me sharply and raises her hand to wave, switching to her best English. I edge behind her as a young man and a woman start up the walk towards us. They are smiling, flashing two sets of glittering white teeth at us from below their sunglasses. I drop my palm from shading my forehead and look down as they reach us.

'Hi, how's it going?' The man reaches out his hand and my mother shakes it. They both take off their sunglasses. The man has green eyes. The woman has blue.

'Thank you,' my mother says awkwardly. I can tell she's nervous. 'Please have a look around.'

The man and woman start walking between the furniture, touching some, leaning down for a closer look at others. The man tests out the dining chairs, sitting on one for a few seconds. I watch them walk around, touching all of our stuff. I try to imagine the table lamp in their house, the man sitting on our armchair in his living room, the woman opening and closing our curtains on her window.

My mother follows them around, holding her hands together, fingers braided through each other, squeezing them so tight that her knuckles are white. Her eyes track them as they move past the dining table, the chairs, the bookcase, the floor lamp. Every time they shake their heads and walk to the next thing, she squeezes her fingers together tighter. Her face looks both excited and angry, and I suddenly feel nervous, too. I start following her, trying to stay inside her shadow as she takes fast little steps.

'Todd, come here,' the woman suddenly calls him from behind the dining table, and turns and disappears behind the bookcase.

'What?' He gets up and goes to her. My mother follows, eager, pressing her hands into fists by her sides so that she stops squeezing them together. One of her nails is still a little purple where she smashed it when she was moving the headboard of her bed outside a few hours ago.

'Are these fantastic or what?' The woman is grinning excitedly, waving the man closer.

My mother suddenly stops dead, frozen at the edge of the garage, and I nearly bump into her.

'Yeah, like, super vintage or something,' the man agrees.

I scoot to the side and look around my mother, peeking from behind the sleeve of her blouse. Everyone is standing very close together, right next to the TV. The man and woman look excited, but my mother is upset, like she doesn't want to give them our TV.

'Uh, I'm sorry, but—' she starts to say, her voice tight, but her English gets bad when she's not happy. I take another step around her so I can see what's happening, and then I realize they aren't looking at the TV.

'How much for these?' The woman turns around to face us, holding up one of the bad plates from the box.

My mother steps forward. 'You don't want these. All broken, not the same set,' she holds up a few to demonstrate. 'See? Not good.'

'But that's why I love them, they have so much character!' The woman gushes. 'Mismatched sets are the new thing.'

My mother keeps staring at her, confused. 'These are bad plates.'

The man laughs. 'How much do you want for them? Would you take twenty?'

'No,' my mother says.

'Is that not enough?' The girl asks.

'You don't understand,' she starts again, but the girl cuts her off. 'They're not for sale?'

'I mean, these aren't for eating,' she manages finally.

'You never ate off of them?'

'No, never.'

'It's okay, we can pay more then, they look like they're in pretty good condition, for being so old, and if you never even ate off of them...' The woman's face is all lit up, and the man is nodding.

'You don't want... anything else?' My mother asks desperately, gesturing to the rest of the furniture.

The woman turns around and the man casts a glance over his shoulder, to be polite, and they both shake their heads. 'Sorry,' the woman says. 'We already have most of this stuff. Really what we need is dinnerware, kitchen things.'

'How about thirty?' The man ups their offer.

My mother looks down at the boxes. I see something change in her face – everything softens and gets droopy, like when she's just woken up from a nap that went too long.

'Come on, let's give her thirty-five,' the man is saying to the woman quietly, both of them huddled together, turned away from us. 'Thirty-five is still a steal,' he looks back to my mother, and smiles again. 'What do you say? We'll give you thirty-five in cash.'

My mother is still looking down at the boxes of bad plates, her eyebrows pushed together. Her lips are moving, but no sound is coming out.

'Is thirty-five okay?' The man looks at the woman, worried it's not enough. He can't tell what she's saying, but I can. She's saying 'bad things always come in threes,' in Chinese. I feel a pounding in my throat, so hard and fast it makes me dizzy.

The woman takes $35 out of her purse and holds it out. 'Final offer,' she holds the money out gently. 'What do you think?'

My mother finally looks up. Her face is blank, smooth and flat like its own kind of plate. 'Thank you,' she says quietly, and the money slips into her hands.

'Fantastic!' The woman squeals, and the man rubs her back and smiles. 'Thank you so much!'

They hoist the boxes into the air and begin to edge their way out of the garage, back toward the car. My mother stares at the money in her hands, as if she's not sure what it is.

'These will look so great when they're stacked up on the shelves over the stove,' the woman is saying to the man as they edge into the sunlight.

'Wait,' my mother shouts suddenly, lurching forward. 'I need to keep two,' she says, desperate.

They look at each other, confused.

'Any two,' she says. 'Please?'

The man shrugs. 'Sure, I guess that's okay. Do you mind if we give you the most chipped ones?'

'Yes, yes, that's fine,' she nods rapidly.

The man takes out two chipped bowls from his box, and hands them to her. They settle into her hands softly, as if they weigh nothing.

I watch them walk away down the end of the driveway, staggering under the weight of the heavy cardboard boxes in their arms. The man balances his box on his thigh, the edge of it resting on the back bumper of their car, and pops the trunk. It jumps open with a squeak, and they ease the boxes in, shifting around the rest of what they've collected earlier this morning from other yard sales – a vacuum, a set of wooden picture frames, a rolled up rug, a clock.

'Thanks again!' The woman waves at us as she ducks in through her door and sits down. The car rumbles to life and she reaches for her seatbelt. 'Good luck with the rest!'

I raise my hand and wave back as the man eases the car away

from the kerb and drives off. A few seconds later, they're gone, and the street is empty again.

'What will we do now if we have bad luck?' I ask softly. We are both standing at the edge of the garage, just inside the shade of the roof, facing out toward the driveway and the front lawn, where all of our stuff is scattered across the concrete and grass, roasting in the sun.

I take the plastic bag of plums out of my pocket and put one in my mouth. I hold the bag up to my mother, to give her the last one, but she doesn't move.

I look up at her. 'Mom?' I say.

She doesn't answer. She is staring at the pair of mismatched, chipped old bowls in her hands, running her fingers over the top one, across the snaking, feathery hairline cracks on its rim. She does this for a long time, so long I don't know how much time has passed, and doesn't say a word. I keep waiting for her to go get a plastic bag from the back of the garage, and tie them up in it and break them, but she doesn't. She just keeps holding the last two bad plates in her hands and staring down at them.

Cages
Joanne L. M. Williams

I didn't decide to be a monster. I didn't even know I was one at first; and sometimes I miss those days. I've never killed anyone, in armour or otherwise, or captured anyone, virginal or otherwise. My family are herbivores. No one ever believes that: I think it's the teeth. Or the scales. But I am a monster; I must be, because here I am in chains in this specially-made dungeon, made for those like me. I came quietly when they brought me here. I almost regret that now; how docile I was then.

When she first came to visit, I believe it was out of boredom. Or perhaps curiosity: I don't suppose she had seen a thing like me before. But she spoke to me. Not at me; she spoke to me. At first our conversation was, as far as I understand these things, fairly trivial. Small talk, but no less pleasant. To be asked who I am, how I am! Well – it's a novelty.

As we grew more used to each other, more comfortable, she stayed longer and talked more. She began to read me stories. I liked that. I tried to tell her a few of my own in turn. And she grew bolder, or fonder, or both. She stroked my snout and told me I was beautiful. She told *me* I was beautiful. She said that my eyes were stars and that my scales shimmered like the sunlight on the ocean. I have never seen the ocean.

Is she beautiful? I wouldn't know how to tell. Princesses have never been my thing. She is kind, and clever, and when she appears things are brighter. One day she kissed me very gently, and then she cried. I didn't understand at first, but I knew that I had failed her. She didn't come back for a week. A whole, terrible, boring, deadly, heart-wrenching week. When she did she cried again, but in a different way. As if she had failed me. It took time that day, but she told me the truth. She had let herself believe that I had been enchanted in some way. That a curse had been placed upon me. In short, that I might be a human prince.

I can't believe she assumed I was a boy. I mean, honestly! But she was my friend and she was sorry; and I forgave her for her foolishness. The next time she came she was serious, but no longer sad.

'We will just find a different way to set you free,' she said. I have to admit it was a beautiful idea. The thought of spreading my wings into flight again, to unfurl, to rise. To simply move where I pleased. The possibility of it was maddening. Wonderful, and beyond belief, of course. Of course. But tantalising. And she was on edge with it too, I could feel it. Why, I wondered, was this of importance to her?

'Because I know what it is like to be in a prison too.' A different look on her face then. Oddly strong; undefeated. Not really a princess look, to the best of my scanty knowledge. Perhaps I have been making assumptions too, all this while.

We carried on as before for a time, though increasingly serious. More stories and confidences shared. There was a strange sweetness about it and I can't deny I enjoyed my time with her. Yet, there was always this pressing, needling sense in me of something bigger and greater that now seemed possible. The almost-promise of freedom in what she said. The image dancing in front of my eyes, which so delighted and frustrated me that I felt I might die.

One day she came and she told me that she had an idea. And her eyes then as she said it; I didn't understand her eyes! They sparkled with an excitement that she would not explain, but beyond that emerald gleam was something sadder and deeper. I cried and I did not know why.

*

I didn't see her again alone. Instead, after some days, some men came and they laughed and said that the princess had taken an odd fancy to me and that I was to be her pet. Instead of this dungeon I was to live in a pretty cage in her apartment. A silk-draped gilded cage. Like her. I was to be moved in time for the coronation of her brother as King. I was to be presented in a parade.

In due course I was tied and hoisted and moved. It was wearying and uncomfortable, because I could not, of course, be permitted to make my way there myself. Instead I had my wings bound, and was in turn tied to a cart, and manoeuvred through corridors not designed for my bulk. Humans can be so impractical! Finally I was placed, well, more or less dumped, onto silk cushions in my – literally – gilded cage. She had better have a good explanation!

And she never explained in words as such, and yet she did explain. She said such cruel things when her attendants were around, but in the brief moments between, when their backs were turned, that look came into in her eye; and a snatched apology was given.

And then the one crucial moment.

Near dawn, us both awake, attendant sleeping. She reaches through those golden bars and to the collar fitted on me. She has a knife and for one terrible moment I think she intends to free me through death. No, she slides it under the collar and cuts almost all the way through the leather from the back. From the front nothing looks amiss, unless you were to get too close; and no one will do that.

The next morning: the parade. Noisy and over-bright, but humans, like everything else, will have their fun. A good number of gasps at my presence, led by her on, I kid you not, a pink silk leash, studded with jewels, attached to the doctored leather collar. I have to admire her style. And it was, I admit, somewhat gratifying, the stir we caused. I found myself craving, enjoying it almost. I saw her toss her pretty dark hair and incline her prettier chin towards the crowd; She felt it too, and was intoxicated like me. We could be so wonderful, so praised. Such a strange sensation, on the point of freedom, to see the beauty of the cage.

She broke the spell, not me. She turned briefly, caught my eye, and said quietly, 'Now.' She turned back, and a few seconds later I felt the sharp tug she gave. I pulled back against her and beat my wings. Underused, and shaky as they were, they did not fail me. The collar snapped and I soared.

Soared up and up and away from it all. Away from her. There were some shouts, but the only one I could pick out was hers. Play-acting to convey her innocence, I conjectured. I hope so; I hope so.

In the wide open sky I dance, giddy on my freedom. This is what I was born for. I may see all the oceans of the world now, and all the lands. I no longer belong to the ground, or the dungeon, or the cage. I no longer belong with her.

I couldn't take her with me, you understand. Just think of the stories that would be told: the dragon capturing the princess! They would hunt us down with their bows and arrows and swords.

But some nights nestling in the snowy mountains I think of her, and I hear that cry. Was I supposed to take her with me? Did I betray her? I do not know, and the not knowing chafes at me like the chains I used to wear. I will go back: I must go back, and so, one night, I do.

She is there on the battlements and she sees me and she doesn't hesitate. 'Just over the gate,' she says, and climbs on. I rise gently, and she clings tightly. It hadn't occurred to me that she might be scared of flying, but she is. Scared, but determined, and brave.

I set her down gently outside of her cage-no-more, and she kisses my snout once again. 'Goodbye.' I beat my wings, stronger now and sure. They catch the air currents, and I move up, higher and higher, and fly to freedom.

Comeback Special
Katy Darby

Mediumship isn't something you do for the money. It's something you can't help doing, and frankly, the pay's crap. That's why I work out of my flat above the Paradise Nail Bar on New Cross Road: I can't afford a proper office. Besides, most of my clientele come to me by word-of-mouth, just like Marina. Marina was younger than my average client, and extremely earnest. She was also very eager to speak to Elvis Presley.

I guessed this because she showed up at 10pm in a copy of Priscilla's wedding dress, clutching two hundred quid in wrinkled twenties. She mentioned the name of a fellow psychic who'd recommended her to me (or the other way round, I suppose) so I sighed, and let her in. Princess Di's more my speciality, but I like a challenge.

'Cup of tea?' I suggested, as she slunk timidly into my receiving room. (It's the spare room really, but done out with lamps and scarves and all the tat people expect.) She slipped through the rainbow plastic bead-curtain, subsiding onto the clients' chair with a sigh. Unlike Elvis, Marina wasn't one of nature's superstars: whereas the King had exuded a confident charm tempered with appealing vulnerability, poor Marina was a nightmare of nerves and nibbled cuticles even the Paradise Nail Bar couldn't have saved.

Like so many of my clients, Marina had lost someone close to her: in this case her Mum, who'd had a colourful youth in America, including a stint as a Las Vegas showgirl in the 70s. Marina had never known her father and never particularly minded, until with her dying breath, Mum told her his name: Elvis Presley. She even had the birth certificate to prove it, sort of. It was from a Vegas hospital, dated 16th February 1978, seven months to the day after the King's death, but the father's name was conspicuously absent. Marina's Mum claimed they'd had a fling in the heady summer of '77, when Elvis was playing the casinos, and this had resulted in Marina.

Imagine! One minute your dad's Nowhere Man: the next he's a rock legend, pop-culture icon and forty years dead. But that last detail wasn't going to stop Marina tracking down her new daddy. Marina lived in Croydon, worked in Peacocks, didn't sing, didn't dance, and had always preferred Johnny Cash. But now, when she looked in the mirror, she sometimes saw the ghost of a sneer on her lips, the hint of a quiff in her thick dark hair, and wondered.

'Since Mum passed, I've read everything I could find,' she said earnestly. 'I've got all the books, all the documentaries, everything, but I still … it's *possible*, that's all I know. I've just got to know if it's *true*. You're my last hope.' She turned pleading hound-dog eyes on me and I thought, *oh shit*.

You see, despite being a fan, I've never actually managed to contact Mr. Presley: Princess Diana and Marilyn I'm quite friendly with, but not Elvis. Marina had been vague over the phone: just talked about getting in touch with her deceased father. Dead parents are usually an easy gig: unless they've got a grudge, they're always keen to hear from the kids. But when she told me the story of the King and the showgirl: well, it was lucky she was paying in cash because otherwise, with my luck, I wouldn't even've tried. Still, for a fistful of twenties… let's just say even spiritualists have to eat.

I dimmed the lights, took her thin hand, closed my eyes and put my head back. I can't really describe what it's like, calling into the beyond with my mind; probing the ether with psychic tendrils. It's sort of frightening and familiar all at once; like walking round your house in the dark. The buzz varies a lot, too. Sometimes it's like a cocktail party over there, and sometimes it's as packed and lonely as a graveyard: plenty of people around but nobody to talk to. We don't call the dead 'the silent majority' for nothing.

Anyway, I hadn't hardly started calling out for Elvis, feeling a right idiot and knowing I'd fail as I always had before, when I felt … well, it's hard to describe. It was like my body was a suit and someone was putting me on. Normally spirits are extremely polite about physical possession: like sensitive lovers or high-end estate agents, they handle you gently, ask permission to enter, then slip in expertly, with minimum fuss. They don't just batter down the door and wipe their boots on the carpet, metaphorically speaking. However, with a spirit you've been trying to contact for years, beggars certainly cannot be choosers.

So I went with it: I let him all the way in.

A kind of gleaming warmth spread through me as he settled into my chair. I felt his desire to speak to Marina almost matched hers to hear him. And I felt something else, too: my upper lip, sneering; my hips snaking in the chair, my toes tapping. I'd never been taken over so completely by a presence before: the King's charm and force of personality worked just as well post-mortem as in life. You can forgive a girl for being starstruck.

'Honey?' he said. His Tennessee-honey accent coming out of my mouth felt strange and wonderful.

'D-daddy?' stammered Marina.

Have you ever watched those shows, you know, the ancestry ones and the ones where they reunite adopted children and birth-parents, the happy ones and the sad ones? Because let me tell you, this reunion was a real tearjerker. Elvis spoke in glowing, tender terms of Marina's mother; her blue eyes, her long legs, her big heart ('How could he *know*?' she gasped.) It was all the usual stuff, I suppose, but it seemed special, somehow.

He said he wished he could've been there for her, and he sent her all his love from the beyond, where he and her grandmother Grace and Uncle Jesse were safe and happy too.

Then he signed off with love, asked her not to take a DNA test because it would break Priscilla's heart to know he'd cheated, and wished her happiness. Marina went away glowing, and I collapsed, excited and exhausted, staring at the sheaf of twenties on the table. I almost didn't want to take her money, given what a thrill it'd been to have the King visit, but cat food doesn't buy itself, so I reached to pocket the notes.

Resistance; my hand skirted around the cash, spidering away.

Like that, is it? I thought. Sick of being bled dry by the Colonel in life, maybe Elvis was hoping to save his daughter the price of a psychic phone call. I willed my hand forward again; it worked this time, but the spirit hiding in my body had already given himself away.

'You're still in there, aren't you?' I said, loudly. My own head nodded, then hung in shame. What on earth was Elvis doing hijacking *me*? Didn't he have better things to do in the afterlife than wander round a South London flat? Or was he (as I was starting to suspect) not who he said he was after all? Wasn't Elvis's Mum called Gladys, not Grace?

Had I, in fact, been possessed by an Elvis impersonator?

I clenched my fists, forcefully unhitched my lip, and marched myself to the mirror, where I stared hard into my own narrowed eyes, seeking out whoever was in there, wrestling me for control.

'Oi you,' I said sternly, 'out! I don't like uninvited guests, especially under false names.' Identity theft is surprisingly common in the spirit world. Usually a bored or lonely presence poses as someone popular and loved: and who's more beloved than Elvis?

'But Ma'am, I'm the man you want!' he protested, in an accent that was starting to sound more Middlesbrough than Memphis. This cheeky bastard had fooled poor Marina, but he wasn't deceiving me.

'Oh yeah?' I said. 'Sing me something.'

My lips in the mirror quivered as he launched into *Love Me Tender*. I stopped him with a single finger laid across my mouth.

'Everybody knows that one,' I said. 'Sing my favourite. Sing *Never Been to Spain*.'

Now, despite being a great song, this isn't part of the average person's Elvis repertoire: only serious fans know he recorded it. As a connoisseur of the King's back-catalogue I know the words – but whoever was squatting in my body clearly didn't. Never been to Spain; he'd probably never even been to Southampton. Just another dead wannabe: and they're the saddest kind, because if anything buggers up someone's lifelong ambitions, it's death.

'All right, you've got me.' A Northern accent now, broad Yorkshire, full of defeat and regret.

'I think you owe me an explanation.' I folded my arms and waited.

'I'm sorry, love,' he said at last. 'It's been such a bloody long time without a peep. None of me mates even realised I was dead for years, and then … well, nobody cared. I never even knew I had a daughter out there – can you imagine? And then when Jean passed over, well, I recognised her at once (you don't forget legs like those) but I couldn't let her see me, in case – I heard she'd told Marina who her dad was with her dying breath. That's why I had to jump in. Talk to Marina first. So she'd never find out.'

'What are you on about?' I said. 'Her Mum had a fling with *Elvis*. Are you calling her a liar, or am I supposed to believe Elvis came from Yorkshire?'

'Neither,' he said. 'And both, sort of … Colonel Tom spotted me in a lookalike contest, took me on as a backing singer and used me as a double after shows, so the King could get away. Jean really did think I was him, all the time we were together. Then he died, and I had to break it off, of course; disappear. Always regretted that; Jean was a wonderful girl. Couldn't show my face at the casino again after doing a runner; didn't have the heart to sing any more. Ended up working at a gas-station in Texas. Never had a wife or a family. Never had anything much, outside music. What could I do?'

'You could not lie to people?' I suggested.

A chuckle rose in my chest. 'Come on love, the King's too busy to take calls. All us impersonators who've passed over, we take 'em instead; we're happy to, and the fans love it. He's like Princess Di, you know? Hounded all his life, now he just wants to be left alone. You won't tell her, will you? Marina, I mean. She really is my daughter. I just wanted to talk to her; just once. But if she finds out her old man was nothing but a tribute act, you'll break her heart.'

Dark, sad eyes stared into mine in the mirror. The cocky Elvis strut had sagged into an apologetic slump. No wonder people still wanted to be him: even I'd been under the spell, for an hour or so. How could I burst Marina's bubble? Who could it hurt, to let her believe?

'Flipping hell,' I said, annoyed with myself for swallowing a sob-story, and even more annoyed that I'd been entertaining fake Dianas all these years, 'all right then. Piss off and I won't tell Marina the truth.'

My head jerked up. My nostrils flared. A lazy, lopsided grin tugged at my mouth. I threw my shoulders back and struck a pose, for all the world as if I were wearing a slightly too-tight jumpsuit, gold sunglasses and a cape. I pointed at myself in the mirror and snapped off a confident wink, full of confidence, promise, personality; magic. And just for a moment, I saw him in my eyes: what Marina's Mum had seen. I saw the King.

'Thank you,' he said. 'Thangyou ver'much.'

And then Elvis left the building.

Destiny's Children
Rosalind Stopps

I found my granddaughter in John Lewis. I'm not a snob, and I wouldn't have minded if she came from the pound shop or Lidl, but she didn't. She was in the Oxford Street John Lewis women's clothes section, in a pram in between Jigsaw and Hobbs and there was no one with her at all. I made faces at her for a while to keep her happy, played peep-bo in between the cashmere jumpers and pretended to sneeze but we were both getting bored and still she hadn't been claimed.

I'm good with babies. In any other age I'd have been sat in a corner somewhere knitting, with grandchildren on my lap and a fire to warm my knees, but I was born in the golden age of rock and roll. I still wear size eight jeans from Top Shop and sleep with at least one new man a month, usually from the internet. I live alone in a penthouse flat and my only daughter does something inexplicable in Silicon Valley to do with picturing the exact size of items when shopping online. She froze her eggs years ago and by the time she defrosts them I'll be dead, nothing more than a photo on a computer, a virtual grandma.

So I'm afraid that when I saw Alberta I was unable to resist helping myself. After all, if her mother or father or grandmother or nanny had wanted to keep her, they would hardly have left her alone in such a public place, would they? And she liked me, I could tell that she did. She held her chubby arms out towards me and she offered me a turn of the small penguin she was holding.

There was no clue to her name in the old fashioned silver cross pram so we chose a new one together. I was prepared to follow the alphabet through to Xanthe, Yolande and Zuleika if necessary but she waved and cooed at Alberta so that was just fine with me. I found out later from the newspaper report that her name had actually been Daisy but Alberta suited her much better so I stuck with it. I'd lived in Canada for a while when I was younger, and it's nice for children to have links with their heritage.

What about her poor mother, I expect you are thinking, wasn't she terribly upset and bereft and all that sort of thing? I guess she was, at first. I have to admit that she was, at least for a while. She gave interviews on TV wearing designer sunglasses and dabbing at her nose but she had another baby the next year and wrote a bestselling book about the whole experience that made her a lot of money. She knew by then, you see. She knew that Alberta was safe, and being looked after. I sent word via a third party, and a substantial amount of cash, and promised to hand her over if either of them got too upset.

'Thank you very much,' she said in the note that she sent back to me. 'I was actually finding life quite difficult and the baby seemed to have insomnia. Also she hated my personal trainer and misbehaved on long haul flights, so I'm happy for her to stay with you, as long as no one, no one ever finds out.'

'That's sorted then, Bertie,' I said. 'Looks like it's just you and me.' She giggled and crawled off to examine the paints I had laid out in the corner, to encourage her creativity. I'd installed a wipe clean area over the floor and halfway up the walls, so whatever mess she made didn't matter. I photographed it each day and planned to put together a mural of photographs showing her development.

My friends were green with envy. They came round more often, drawn by Bertie's youth and gorgeousness as if it might rub off on them. They held her reverently, as if she was a religious relic or the last surviving baby in the world.

'The future of the human race depends on this little poppet and her friends,' said Maria.

I thought that she said 'prophet' for a moment. I had known

Maria vaguely before Bertie, but never as a close friend. She visited often now and this time she had brought an expensive bear and tales of how she hoped her son would settle down soon.

'He's gay,' she said, 'but quite settled with his partner, and they have a dog. That's a good sign, isn't it, having a dog?'

I loved that they thought I might be some kind of oracle, someone who might know about such things.

'Did your daughter have a dog, before she had this sweet little thing?'

I smiled in a sad way to show that no, my daughter had not dabbled in canine ownership before launching into motherhood.

Yes, I'd told everyone that Alberta was my daughter's child. It was a long time since my daughter had visited, and I thought that by the next time she came I would have thought of a plan. If that sounds stupid, let me put it another way. I was in love, that's the beginning and the end of it. I'd fallen for this child just as surely as if she had been propelled from my elderly vagina after a miracle sexagenarian pregnancy featured exclusively in the Daily Mail. I just wanted to be with her, and I couldn't think logically, couldn't imagine further than the next five seconds. Think of the most powerful crush you've ever had and double it. No, quadruple it. That's how I felt about Bertie.

We worked out a rota. It wasn't exactly a babysitting rota, because I rarely left the house apart from when I took Bertie for her afternoon walk. More of a company rota. One of my friends would keep me company at all times, passing the nappy cream and making tea until I felt quite royal. Sometimes there were two of them at a time, especially in the afternoon when we took a turn around the park, one on either side of the pram.

'Is she warm enough?' someone would say, or, 'let me get her an extra cardigan, it's a bit nippy today.'

I was in heaven. I remembered how lonely I had been, not only when my own daughter was little but recently too, and I marvelled at how things had changed.

It was at least three months before the questions started, but once they started, they escalated like a spring storm.

'When's your daughter coming back, did you say?' and, 'I'm sure she won't be wanting to leave her lovely baby much longer.' That kind of thing.

I invented several business deals that needed to be made by my daughter in person, two relationship traumas and a dodgy appendix. I began to think that I would have to use a more long term illness to explain her continued absence, a psychiatric one this time. I was glad of the helpers as I researched all weekend on the internet, barely seeing my beloved Bertie apart from at bedtime. I am a quick learner though, and by Monday morning I had committed all the symptoms of manic depression to memory. I was going to drop them into my conversations a little at a time until my listeners formed their own conclusions, it was best that way. Unnecessary tears, that's where I was going to start. I was ready, and feeling quite sad about the tragic story, when the doorbell rang. The rota said that Frances was coming. She was one of my older friends and I always enjoyed spending time with her, so I decided to start laying down clues.

I didn't get a chance. I opened the door and they were all there, all seventeen of my grandma friends, clustered round the door like carol singers.

'I'm the spokeswoman,' said Maria. 'We need to talk.'

They bustled past me and filled my living room, some standing, some sitting. I held on tight to Bertie even though she was trying to leap into the arms of several of her favourites.

'She isn't your granddaughter, is she?' said Maria.

Some of them gasped, as if this was further than they would have ventured. I kept my mouth closed. If I didn't say anything, I couldn't say the wrong thing. I clutched hold of Alberta until she squealed in alarm. I couldn't bear it if they took her away, I know I couldn't. I would have to go back to Pilates and wine and unsuitable men. I started to cry.

'Maria, let me say it,' said Frances. 'You're frightening her.'

She handed me a tissue and I blew my nose, which always made Bertie laugh.

'The thing is,' said Frances, 'we want one too. Well, not one between us, one each really. We need grandchildren, and we need them now, before we get senile or unfit or both. You have to help us.'

I stopped crying.

'For real?' I said.

'Look,' one of the others said. I think it was Carol, and she held up a beautifully knitted lace shawl. 'Look, I've got this made and ready, but none of my kids can afford a baby.'

Other women began to produce pieces of knitting and sewing in a rainbow of colours, thrusting them towards me as if by touching them I could make them less empty, more full of life.

'I don't know,' I said but I did know, of course I did. I was already planning the first one, which I hoped would be for Frances.

Bringing up babies is difficult work, and young people have a lot on their plates. What could be more natural than leaving it to us oldies to raise the next generation?

There's quite a few of us now. We hang out in John Lewis and other posh shops, and we've branched out into nice cafés and upmarket festivals. We choose carefully. Alberta has a little brother called Darius and a couple of the grandmas even have twins. We've got so famous that the mums leave a sign in the prams – a small bear wearing a hat. If we see a hatted bear we know that the parent (usually the mum) could do with a break, and we take the baby away. Not all the mums want them back, but that's ok too. We've installed a ticket system like they have at the deli counter. If your number comes up and you don't want the baby on offer, you have no other chances, and everyone knows that. It has worked well so far.

Someone pointed out recently that we needed a name to

make us feel more of a unit. We meet up a lot, in each other's houses and in the parks, but it's good to have a name for the headed paper. I wanted Pussy Riot or something modern but several of the older members worried that it could be offensive, so we went for Destiny's Children.

I think that makes it clear.

Smoking Ban
Jennifer Rickard

Gladys was upset. No, not upset, angry. Gladys was angry. And when Gladys got angry, people got roasted.

She eyed the cowering messenger, plumes of smoke drifting from her nostrils. 'Say that again,' she demanded.

The snivelling messenger snivelled. 'Th–there's a ban on smoking, ma'am. You can't have any cigarettes. The king ordered it. He said it was all terribly bad for us and that we would all live much better lives if we partook in some refreshing herbal tea rather than poisoned our lungs with foul smoke and grime – begging ma'am's pardon – so he just... banned them. The city's civilians are no longer allowed to smoke.'

Gladys let the 'ma'am' slide. People just didn't know how to speak to dragons these days. And at least he hadn't mentioned the paradox of an animal that could naturally breathe fire and smoke requesting two hundred Marlboro in its next hoard from the city. 'I'm not a civilian,' she snarled.

'W–well you sort of are, I mean you're on all the flags and everything–'

'I am,' Gladys said very calmly, 'a fucking dragon. I am a fucking dragon going through cold turkey and a dragon going through cold turkey is not a happy dragon, got it, bitesize?'

The messenger shook from head to toe but stood his ground. Gladys was faintly impressed. 'I'm sorry, ma'am. He says you can have more goats if you want, in recompense.'

He waved a hand at the already unfortunate creatures standing by Gladys's cave with the rest of the hoard. One of them bleated plaintively.

Gladys reached forward and hooked a claw under the

messenger's shirt, dragging him closer to her steaming nose. 'Tell you what, cupcake. I'm going to let you live just so you can go back and tell your measly mouthful of a king that he has made a *big* mistake. All right?'

She smiled, showing rows of teeth, some with rotting goat flesh still stuck between them. The messenger squealed. Gladys nodded grimly. Message received.

The quivering messenger eventually reported something about the dragon not being a happy turkey and goats wanting cigarettes, once he could be made to speak without screaming that is, but the king got the gist anyway. He sat back in his throne, said 'Pssh,' and moved on to the next topic.

That night, the king's daughter went missing.

Gladys wasn't quite sure how to handle her new hostage. The princess was blonde, pretty and so skinny that there would barely be any point eating her, which was all par for the course when it came to princesses, but she'd also reacted very oddly to being kidnapped.

When Gladys had turned up, she'd merely sighed and reached for her bag, then passively allowed Gladys to pluck her from her room with one deft claw without screaming for the guards once. She'd actually *yawned* during the resulting flight over the kingdom and when they'd reached the cave, she'd just said, 'Some throw cushions in here could really brighten the place up,' and fallen asleep neatly in a corner. And now she was sitting by the entrance to the cave and embroidering. And singing the sort of songs that made birds sit on her shoulders and fluffy bunnies pop randomly into existence.

Gladys tapped her claws irritably on a nearby rock. She wanted a cigarette.

'Look, shouldn't you be panicking or something?' she snapped at last. She didn't really make a habit of talking to her hostages – it would be a bit like striking up a conversation with the steak on your plate – but she was curious and fed up and nicotine deprived.

The princess raised her perfectly perfect head. 'Should I be?'

Gladys rolled her yellow eyes. 'You *are* being held hostage by an angry dragon.'

The princess shrugged. 'Yes, but you won't actually hurt me. You'll keep me here for a while, then my prince will turn up, slay you in a terrific battle and carry me off to safety. And then we'll get married and live happily ever after. Everyone knows that.'

Gladys grinned. 'I'd like to meet the prince who could slay me.' Several had tried in her lifetime, but you didn't become a grown dragon these days without learning a few prince-slaying techniques. Her favourite trick was to hover over them and bite their heads off while they were still reaching for their oh-so-shiny swords.

The princess tossed back her swathe of blonde hair. 'He will. You'll see.'

Gladys snorted. 'What's going to happen is that your king is going to crack like the nut he is and give me two hundred Marlboro for your safe return.'

The princess sighed pityingly. 'Have you ever thought about replacing cigarettes with carrot juice?'

'Oh my God,' said Gladys, and went deeper into the cave to terrorise some goats.

But she couldn't stay away. It had to be the lack of nicotine. It was making her fixate on things. That and the fact that the princess was mad as a box of monkeys. She sat on her rock by the cave entrance from dawn to dusk, embroidering steadily the whole time. She sang constantly, with a host of birds to sing back to her. She petted the goats and treated them so kindly that Gladys almost felt guilty for eating them. She even rearranged the rocks around the cave to improve the Feng Shui, whatever that was. And she chatted at Gladys – God, how she *chatted*. You couldn't shut her up. She went on and on about how amazing her life was going to be when the prince turned up, how happy they'd be together, what a joyous existence she would have. Meanwhile the days stretched on and there was no prince on the horizon.

'Look,' Gladys said at last. 'How about instead of waiting for the prince to rescue you, you just ran out of the cave while I was distracted? It would be really easy, you're already sitting right by the entrance.'

The princess looked offended. 'But the prince has to save me.'

'You could just save yourself,' Gladys suggested, but the princess had started singing again and those bloody raucous birds successfully drowned Gladys out.

She was baffling, Gladys decided. She really was.

'Do you ever eat *anything* with vitamins in it?' the girl asked one day, once Gladys had finished devouring the doomed goat of the day and was lazily picking bits of flesh out of her teeth with a claw.

'Don't need to,' Gladys said, feeling pleasantly full and thus inclined to chat. 'I'm a dragon.'

The princess sniffed. 'I'm just saying, it's not good for you. Your chakras will get all clogged. And look what all that blood has done to your claws!'

Gladys stared at her claws. They were a bit of a mess, but then they always were.

'Have you ever even had a manicure?' The girl sighed and fished around in her bag, bringing out some equipment. 'Right, give me a paw.'

Gladys, nonplussed, obeyed. Five minutes later, her claws were red with nail polish instead of blood. She wasn't sure what to think about this.

'There,' said the princess, sounding pleased. 'Perfect. You look great.'

Gladys examined her new shiny talons. She supposed it didn't look too bad.

One night, when the princess was huddling amongst the rocks and blathering on about what type of cake would be served at her wedding, Gladys interrupted. 'What about afterwards?'

'After what?' asked the human morsel.

'After the wedding,' Gladys said. 'What do you do after that? How do you spend your days?'

The princess stared at her. 'Well, I – well, I wait to become Queen, I guess.'

'Yes, and while you're doing that?'

'Um.' The princess gazed blankly at the cave wall for a while. 'I suppose I could embroider.'

'But you embroider now,' pointed out Gladys.

'So?'

'Well, if all I was going to do after I got married was embroider, I'd make sure I did something else before then.'

The girl blinked at her. 'Like what?'

'Like...' Gladys cast around for an activity. 'Like travel, I suppose. There are lots of interesting places to see besides this one.'

'Are there?' asked the princess. 'I've never travelled.'

'I've travelled all too much,' Gladys bemoaned. 'Dragons tend to. We're not very welcome guests.'

The princess shuffled a foot in the dirt. 'So where have you been?'

Gladys told her. She found herself telling all of it, the years and years spent flying around different countries, just finding a nice warm cave and then getting unceremoniously thrown out of it by locals with pitchforks or stupid, shiny knights. She talked about cities she had seen, mountains, seas, fiery volcanoes, great creaking glaciers, hot wet jungles, dry arid deserts. She talked about snow, and monsoons, and fog, and what it was like to fly above the clouds.

She talked about it all and the princess sat there and listened to every single word.

Of course the prince turned up. He was bound to eventually. Gladys peeked out of the cave distrustfully.

'He's late,' she said. 'And oh my God, he's *glistening*.'

Glistening was the perfect word for what the prince was doing. He glistened from head to toe, from his shimmering hair to his glittering boots. Then he smiled and his teeth could have outshone the sun. Only five hours with a hygienist and a tooth whitening machine could have produced such teeth as those.

'Bloody hell,' Gladys said. 'And you're marrying *that?*'

The princess peeked out of the cave and giggled. 'He does look very eager.'

Gladys grunted. 'He's still late though. All right then, go on.'

The princess stared at her. 'Aren't you meant to go and have a massive battle where he slays you in a gory and grisly fashion?'

Gladys shrugged. 'Don't feel like being slain today. You might as well just go. I don't really want the cigarettes anymore anyway.'

The princess paused. 'Oh. Right.' She hesitated again. 'Look, I made this. For you.'

She presented Gladys with a piece of cloth, on which was a beautifully embroidered dragon smoking a cigarette. Gladys looked down at the cloth and was horrified to discover her vision was blurring. She blinked hastily.

'Bye then,' said the princess, and went out of the cave, picking her way down the rocks to her glistening beloved.

Gladys looked around the cave. It suddenly felt very empty.

The proposal was beautiful, the wedding was beautiful, and everyone agreed that they were a very beautiful couple. The prince was very courteous and kind and oh-so-shiny, and all the court was in raptures over the occasion. All in all, it was everything the princess had dreamed of and more and she enjoyed every moment.

Until, one day, once the excitement of the festivities had passed, she found herself sitting down again with her needle and thread.

Gladys sighed and looked over her collection of goats. There would barely be enough to last the winter and anyway, this cave was feeling emptier and emptier by the day. Maybe it was time to move on.

Just then, she heard a very familiar voice shouting her name. She stuck her head out of the cave entrance. The princess was standing there, grinning.

'I've never been to a jungle,' she said. 'I hear there are monkeys there. And I'd love to see a volcano erupt. And do you think we could climb around on a glacier?'

Gladys stared.

'Oh,' said the princess. 'Also, I brought you some cigarettes. I stole them from the prince.'

She held up the pack victoriously. Gladys smiled.

Desperately Seeking Hephaestion

Elizabeth Hopkinson

(Inspired by *The Family of Darius before Alexander* by Paolo Veronese)

Plato once said that each of us is a man divided, always seeking his other half. I suppose this is what Aristotle was thinking of when he called Alexander and me, 'one soul residing in two bodies'. The question is: whose soul? That's what I've always wanted to know.

In the early days, we had a lot of fun. Back when we used to hang in the Palazzo on the Grand Canal. We used to swap clothes on a regular basis. Then we'd trade places and bite our cheeks to avoid giggling as viewers stared at the painting in bafflement.

'But which one is Alexander?' they'd say.

When they'd gone, we would bend double with laughter, holding onto one another and wiping our eyes.

Only later did the question sink in. *Which one is Alexander?* Never: *which one is Hephaestion?*

After a while, Alexander got bored. He was like that. *Let's conquer India. Let's go to Sogdia.* Too much was never enough for him.

'Everyone says we look like twins. And so we are. Twin souls.' He seized me by the shoulders and kissed me. 'You, too, are Alexander.' His eyes sparkled with mischief. 'Let's make more twins. It'll be fun.'

First we gave Darius's daughters matching dresses. It was a pretty gesture, but not bold enough for Alexander. So we began making doubles of people in the crowd. Not all at once. We spaced it out over time, so that new generations would discover two figures where once there had only been one. Two plumed soldiers. Two observers in turbans. Two androgynous youths –

that to my mind looked worrying like Bagoas – dressed in green and coral. Alexander even gave them twin dogs.

'Look, Hephaestion!' he would say. 'Our sweet twinship reflected everywhere!'

But I began to have my doubts. In all our years, he had never once said, 'I, too, am Hephaestion.' How could I know he didn't multiply twins as he had once multiplied Alexandrias, for his own glory. *These people, too, are Alexander. You are all Alexander.*

My doubts grew when the dwarf and the monkey appeared. Before that, it had been a dark and a fair child, peeping at one another around my legs. That, I could accept. But the dwarf seemed to look on the monkey with horror, as if to say: 'Don't you dare consider me a twin.' I recalled Alexander's words to Darius: 'I am king of all Asia. Do not speak to me as an equal.' From that day, I stood just a fraction further off.

And then he appeared. The child in red. Looking up at Alexander from the safety of Sisygambis's arms. The same cloak and tunic; the same curly hair. A boy made in his own image.

The Great Alexander had succeeded in making himself a new twin. All the hurt of the centuries came flooding in like the Indus. It was as it had been in life. First Bagoas, then Roxane. Always the next conquest, the new horizon. And I was as I had always known myself to be. Expendable. Insignificant.

He didn't even see me leave. Too busy flaunting his magnanimity to Darius's wife and mother. I stood on the polished floor of the gallery and read the title of the painting: *The Family of Darius before Alexander.* Bitter tears came to my eyes. *Before Alexander.* Never mind that the whole point of the story was that Sisygambis had knelt to me. That she had called me, 'Great King,' when she begged for clemency. That for one moment I had known what it was to have the adulation Alexander had imbibed with his mother's milk. No. Who would come to see a painting called: *The Family of Darius before Hephaestion?* What storyteller would speak of Hephaestion the Great? If they spoke of me at all, it would only be as another Alexander, an extension of his all-conquering ego.

I turned my back and walked away.

'This way!'

A voice echoed through the maze of rooms. A sound of footsteps drew nearer. I flattened myself against the marble doorway, hidden by shadows.

'But why does it have to be here?' said a second voice. 'Can't you just say it?'

I could see them now. Two young men in their twenties. One held the other by the wrist, dragging him towards *The Family of Darius*. They were laughing, breathless. I knew the look in their eyes. I had seen it in the eyes of Alexander, time without number. Late at night, outside his tent. Across a crowded council chamber. By my bedside as I lay dying. My throat tightened.

'It has to be here.' The first youth dragged his companion to stand before the enormous canvas, right where I had been standing moments before. 'In front of the painting. Our painting.'

'Very well.' The second youth's lips quirked a smile. He knew what was coming.

'Will you…' His lover took a breath. 'Will you m... Oh God, where's Hephaestion?'

They turned to stare at the painting, now spectacularly empty of – well – me. Viewed from this side, my absence left an awkward gap. Darius's family gazed at a portion of canvas between Alexander and a dull blank. The two little boys played peek-a-boo around nothing. And were those – could those be – tears on Alexander's cheek?

The first youth was shaking.

'It's not possible. I mean, why? Hephaestion and Alexander, that's the whole point. How could they even…?'

'It's all right.' His beloved laid a hand on his shoulder. 'There'll be some explanation. Restoration work or something. Let's go and ask someone.'

The first youth continued to look back in disbelief as his beloved led him away. My cheeks burned with shame. I had done this. To these two, the painting had become a precious symbol of their love, and I had ruined it. How many more like them had there been down the ages? How many more were still to come? Without me, there was nothing for them to hold onto. Without me, the painting was meaningless.

Quietly, I slipped back between frame and canvas. Alexander was waiting. The force of his hug winded me as our breastplates clashed.

'Where were you?' His voice was hoarse. 'I thought you'd left me again.'

'Just getting a change of scenery,' I said. 'Seeing things from a new perspective.'

'Well, don't.' He squeezed my hand. 'I die without you, Hephaestion. You know that.'

I squeezed back. It was good to feel this way again. It had been a long time.

I grinned. 'Let's swap clothes again.'

Alexander's eyes sparkled. They had had that same spark just before he charged up the bank at Granicus. I wanted to kiss each of them a thousand times.

'I was hoping you'd ask,' he said. 'The red looks much better on you. And look!' He pointed. 'I made you a little twin.'

Joy
Julia Kent

I am not really reading. I'm thinking about my bag. I didn't know if I should bring it. I thought it might be presumptuous – embarrassingly so – to think if everything goes well then we'd do it tonight. But to not have it would be worse. If he wanted to… and I couldn't. An opportunity missed. He might be put off. And then, disappointed, never contact me again. I don't know if I could go back to trawling the site. So I brought it, and now I'm looking past my book at it, and worrying it's too obvious. If I were the sort of person who carried a handbag this wouldn't be a problem. The bag-for-life is just too… orange.

'Twenty-seven?'

I wait, as if finishing my sentence. Take a deep breath and then look up from the book.

'Yes.' TwentySeven is my profile name. We've agreed not to use our real names.

'I'm Glen.'

Oh.

'Sorry,' says Glen. 'Do you mind so much? I just… that other name doesn't really feel like me.'

I can't help it. My eyes flick up and down him, from the wispy blond hair to the jeans with the crease down the middle. He guesses what I'm thinking, and colours slightly.

'Silly, I suppose. It was a play on words. My surname's Knight.'

He laughs. Around his embarrassment, he has an unnerving cheeriness. 'I suppose I shouldn't have told you that, either. Not doing very well, am I?'

I don't tell him my real name, which is as inapt a description of me as his username is of him. I do kick the bag-for-life so it's partially hidden under my chair. I'm looking for someone who'll stick to their word. Someone I can trust.

Glen Knight sits down and calls the waiter. Orders hot chocolate and a scone, takes off his fleece.

'So! Have you met any other people from the site?'

He seems unbothered by mentioning the circumstances that led us here. I thought maybe we'd ignore them. Pretend our relationship started here, in this John Lewis café, not with five alternately terse and chirpy messages sent over the space of three days.

'No.' I say. Which is true. I haven't met anyone else. I did talk to rufus70 online for about a month, but when I suggested meeting up, in response I received a LOLcats picture telling me I actually could NOT haz cheezburger, from which I deduced I'd been duped by teenagers. How I laughed. Actually, I did laugh. But when Glen contacted me, I said straight away, let's meet.

'Me neither,' Glen says. 'I don't think anyone really liked the sound of me.'

The cheeriness flickers.

'I'm sure it's not that,' I find myself saying. 'I'm not sure very many people use that site.'

He's back to full wattage. 'You're right!' he says. 'It is a bit niche.'

He pronounces it 'nee-shay'. I can't help but smile. Encouraged, he smiles back. Reflected in his glasses I see my own image. Hair I've cut myself. Skirt I've made myself. Too thin. Pinched. Hungry-looking. I see my smile wavering.

'I'm glad we've met.' I say, quickly.

'Oh, me too.' He sits forward a little, starts to say something. He's interrupted by the waiter, bringing over a mug and plate. Glen takes both and with the largesse of people in our situation, gives the waiter a fiver and says 'keep the change.'

The waiter smiles. 'That'll be six pounds twenty. Sir.'

Glen Knight colours slightly, mutters something about

London prices, and fishes two coins out of his pocket. The waiter leaves.

'Some people just do this over the computer, you know.'

I do know this. I find the thought horrific. 'Yeah,' I say.

'Sky each other. Or whatever. I couldn't do that. If someone won't meet you – how do you know they're for real? That they're actually interested.'

He leans forward again. 'I heard – sometimes? You get two people, on the computer. Both get ready but only one person does it. The other person... just likes to watch.'

I don't believe him. And then I do. Eventually, I believe in everything.

'That's horrible,' I say.

'That's people for you,' he replies, sitting back. 'You can't trust anyone.' Slurps his hot chocolate. And then, 'But I trust you,' he says. 'You're really interested, aren't you? You really want to do it.'

Given what he's just told me, this is crazily naïve. I've done nothing to warrant this. The fact that I am not someone out to dick him around is not something he can assume from the fifteen minutes we've spent together. Or maybe he can, insists something inside me. Maybe he can see it in me. Maybe this bespectacled little man with the bad hair is actually incredibly perspicacious.

'Yes,' I say.

'Thought so. Why? Why do it this way?'

I sit back, away from him. My foot kicks my bag, under the table. He seems to sense my awkwardness.

'Me, I was diagnosed with cancer. Terminal.' He says it quickly. Then, just as quickly. 'I'm not wasting your time. Misdiagnosed with cancer, it turns out. Mixed up with some poor kid in Matlock. Just found out. But, in the meantime, I'd told the wife–'

'The *wife*?'

'–the best friend, the dog. Signed over the house, the accounts. Made it easy for them, you know. Told them to get on with their lives.'

He pauses for a moment. Worries a raisin out of his scone and pops it in his mouth.

'That's what they did. Her and him. Got on. They think I don't know. Think they've managed to keep it a secret. But they're so excited. Even just waiting, like they are now. It's like someone's put light bulbs in their eyes. Instead of... their eyes.'

'You haven't told them you're ok?'

'She was never that happy with me. Not like she is with him. It's better for everyone if I just... find another way. I'm used to the idea now, to tell you the truth. More curious about what it'll be like than anything else. But I don't want to be alone.'

He looks up from his scone. 'You think that's pathetic.'

'No I don't.' I really don't. 'You love her. I don't think I've ever loved anyone. Or been loved.'

He breathes through his nose. A kind of sad huff.

'Gosh,' he says. 'That's why you're on the site? Now that's pathetic.'

I feel my face twist, and my throat catch fire, then see a broad grin break across his. He's joking. It surprises me into a laugh, like I've been punched in the stomach.

'Well. Shall we?' he says, tipping his head back for the last of his drink.

'What?'

'I've got a hotel room,' he says. 'Save the cleaning up. You know – in case it's messy.'

I think about what is in my bag and suspect that it will indeed be messy.

'Just like that?'

'Only if you want to,' he says. And looks away from me, so I can make up my mind.

I think that I don't want to be alone, either. I look at him, at the halo of wispy hair, and the eyes with their kind crinkles. At this man, who is asking me to go with him, who needs me, perhaps. I think about how lonely I have been, and how it has felt, these past months, as if I can't go on. And I decide.

I pick up my bag.

Inside are the instructions I printed off from the website. 'DarkAndStormy, John Lewis, 6.30.' is written at the top, in blue biro. With my other hand I take Glen's.

'Shall we?' he says, again.

'Yeah,' I say. 'We shall.'

At the Bottom of the Sea of Troubles
Lucy Ribchester

When I think of him, it starts with his shoes. Italian leather, I can tell from the tongues. He must have been friends with a sailor to have acquired them, because I can also tell by the way he holds his legs that he is horseman rather than seafarer.

He wears black stockings. His breeches are short, shorter than the fashion, but they suit him. As does the collar, stiff, square, lovely white and gaping as if he has ridden carelessly through some forest. Which he may well have done for all I know. I always remember the mischief in his face, as he stood staring through the menagerie bars at a long-necked thick-lashed ziraph, like he could just get on its back and spur it away.

A poet then? The way he looked at ships, at the section of the Thames that broadened; it was with a hunger that I haven't seen in any sailor.

'Is it yours?'

I thought for a moment he meant the beast and was mocking me. But when he didn't laugh I saw he was pointing at the shop. How I could have taken his money for that great-necked animal of Africa and run, and sometimes in my more bitter moments I wish I had. Then at least I'd have a shilling to show in return for the gifts I've given him.

When we are adrift in the nightless Arctic, I think of the chill on the first night when he made us sit at an outside table in the beer gardens, so that he could watch the ships. Back then I was a boy to him; he paid more attention to the skippers, asked them about light and coastline and birds.

'Eyasses,' one of them said, of the baby hawks we carried back from Arabia to sell to falconers. He liked the word. 'Little eyasses.' He said it over and over.

I saw his currency then.

When would I have time to love him? Not there in the docks, where the ships gave off a stink of whaleskin and tar and men too long alone. Not in the liberties where we walked, under the Ludgate, or in the sorry gaze of pitched traitors' heads stuck on spikes. Devils, watching.

And then I was at sea once more, in my slops and my own Italian shoes I'd bartered for a basket of English wool. When he waved me goodbye after that first meeting he said, 'How can you sail, so uncertain, into the night? Into sea creatures, renegados, pirates?'

I tried to disguise a shiver as a shrug and said, half looking over my shoulder at a boisterous group of men trying on masks, 'Let he that hath the steerage of my course direct my sail.' I looked up to God just as one of the men from the fiesta slapped another on the shoulder and shouted, 'On lusty gentlemen!'

The next time I saw my poet I wasn't even off the bow of the ship. He seemed a fixture there at the Wapping docks, staring like he was cast in black iron; a painted marble man. This way, I later learned, he soaked everything in. He gave away nothing, kept it all, turned it into precious words to sell. I wondered if he ever slept or where his chambers were or when he rehearsed the plays he spoke so shyly of.

Time stands still when you snatch gusts of it in other countries, their time, their different way of walking, talking, smelling. The rest spent on a blank sea grey page, a mute clock with nothing but the edge of the earth on all sides. So you wonder how it is that people move on back home.

His ruff was flashier this time. Square and bright as a pearl, and the corners high, almost reaching into the ginger fleece of his beard. The sailors of course don't follow fashions. They change when it pleases them. Something Spanish today, black lace, a gaudy pin, a crucifix complete with a man on it, to be worn near the heart. Or German trousers, looser, covering to the knees. The sailors don't follow fashions because we are the fashions.

Oh he recognised me. I knew from his eyes. 'I'm parched,' I said. It was true, my voice was filthy salty.

'I can counter that.'

Somehow it was easier to talk this time, shored up in a bankside tavern drinking cheap sherry. 'Yes of course I've been to Syracuse.'

'And Venice?'

'Yes.'

'Tell me what the merchants wear there.'

I described it all. I told him about Castle Elsinore, where we delivered a pair of peacocks that later I heard tell froze to death in the cold grounds.

'And were you ever in a storm?'

'Oh yes, the roughest. My ship was shattered. We were picked up by a galleon who turned out to be benevolent plunderers.' How did he know what of this I fabricated?

'And you plundered with them?'

'They would approach a ship from behind the wind,' I said. 'You won't appreciate how hard that is to do.' He looked put out. 'Dame fortune has an outrageous streak in her, to turn favour when it pleases.'

'Well,' he said, 'she's a woman, isn't she?'

I went on. 'They had no muskets, no cannons. But more skilled marksmen you could never imagine. They used whalegut slings, and bone arrows they'd filed down. They'd aim for the skipper's heart, or the first mate. That way no damage was done.'

We walked late and the evenings blurred into one. He blindfolded me and spun me, and I only knew where he'd led me when I smelled the sawdust and heard wood creak. And it reminded me so much of being in the underbelly of a ship; sailing through worlds, drifting into somnambulance in green mists and waking up somewhere the words and dreams were different.

'The theatre,' I said. 'We're in the theatre.'

'No,' he corrected me. 'We're in the Globe.'

As he unfastened the ribbon behind my head his fingers were clumsy and nearly knocked my cap off, and later I found he'd left a smear of ink hardening in my hair.

We were in the tiring house, and as soon as I clapped eyes on those rows of silk and lace and floor-length French velvet costumes I saw what it was possible to become. He reached into the rack and wrestled out a thick cochineal brocade dress, stiffened into a flat waistband at the stomach, panniered at the hips. 'Try this.' He saw me hesitate. 'Go on, you'll fit. It's meant for a boy.'

'Can I try the bishop's robe instead?' How coy could I sound? Instead of terrified.

He reached across to my brow, pressed his palm flat, then smoothed it. There was curiosity in his eyes. I felt for a moment like a pebble or trinket, like the ziraph he had looked at with mischief. 'I cannot imagine fatigue here,' he said. 'A flaw, a wrinkle.'

I swallowed.

'All right,' he said. 'The bishop's robe.'

He helped me into it, and his hands, his inky hands, lingered at my collar.

And I burned.

Then there was the time we rescued a brown bear. There was a pit across the way from the Globe. It was after a baiting, and the thing was half stuck through a gap in the fence, weals on its paws and a broken scream. He hoisted me up over – 'you're a brave boy' – to push from behind. With sticks to guard us, for the poor thing didn't know if we were friend or foe, we yanked and shoved it, still on its chain, 'til its claws found purchase in the outer wood, its belly snuck through the fence, and plop, it was ours.

'What in the name of God and the devil,' he said, 'am I to do with a bear?' He examined its mangy scarred face. Its eyes were remarkably human.

'Put it in one of your plays.'

We tore along the bank of the river, from Southwark to Lambeth, hair streaming. I had the chain in one hand, and the bear pursued us.

Six months at sea. When I returned this time, the salt and the sun had left their mark and I was both scrawny and dun.

He was there, staring. Every day, he said, he'd come. My hand was the first thing he touched. 'What do you smell of?'

I was ready not to hide any longer.

'Perfume,' I said. 'Arabian perfume.'

When he met my eyes it was with new understanding.

I don't know whether the rooms we went to were his. There was another man there at first, sitting on the bed. They exchanged a few words until the man got up, selected a volume from the shelf and closed the door behind him.

I started with my shoes. Slipped my feet free. Then breeches, stockings, shirt, until I was in my shift; a vain silken piece I always wore right next to my body, to keep the scent close. To remind me every day that I am a woman.

I took away my cap, the pins from my dense black curls. He said nothing. Not even when I was bare-breasted in front of him.

He had on a starched ruff that day and I remember he struggled to take it off. The rest of his finery was easy in comparison, slid away like sealskin. He was paler than me, much paler, and the ginger in his beard threaded down his body, now gold, now dark. I couldn't think of words to describe him, but he made me think of all the sweet things I had ever tasted, touched or seen. An oyster, freed from its shell, apricots in hazy coats, damson flesh. A tall elk standing in the snow.

Afterwards, he took up my shift and slipped it on, widening the straps at his shoulders. I wore his stockings and the iced lace ruff, and we lay moulded by the threads of each other's fabric. Bound.

I went to his play, noted the reference to Elsinore, to slings and arrows. Told him. He smiled, as if that were reward enough.

It was only when we were casting off, and I was back in my slops and jacket, sea-ready, steeled for a voyage to the Arctic, that the skipper said, 'Don't see so much of Will these days.'

I kept my smile tight, a locket, locked in my heart.

'Still, I s'pose his wife must want him some of the time. Back home. S'pose she sees less of him than some of the sailors' molls. Oh yes, and his three bonnie children, too. Can't remember their names.'

My heart fell out of me then, pierced, down into the dockside grit. And I never picked it back up.

When I look down upon that blank grey page that rocks in opposition to the ship, I think how desperate and beautiful and how strange it would be to extinguish into nothingness, melt into it like the elusive flame inside an emerald.

Slings and arrows. But better to be at the bottom of this sea than floating on the sea of troubles we toss ourselves to back on land.

I stare until I make a mirror. I see both a young boy and a dark lady. And my rage is not for the lie, the terrible lie he told, or the truth he didn't mention, or his double love. But for the things he took from me; words, objects, stories. Gave back nothing in return. Where am I in all the body of his work?

I take off one shoe then the other – shoes that will forever link me to him in my mind. Unslip my shift from my shoulders and pull it off through my shirt. The threads that took his odour and his heat. I stuff it tight into the toe of one shoe, bind both together with sea rope, and in the tongue of the other I leave a note; 'Love is such stuff as dreams are made on.'

I bind them and I throw them.

And of course I hope that they will float on currents back to him. But instead they eddy only for a second, then sink, pulled down, spiralling until they are a speck of cloudy mist.

We/She
J. A. Hopper

We are all *She*, all 3,117 of us; itemised, docketed and accounted for in a mothballed warehouse just outside Milton Keynes. Our puffy caramel blonde hair, waved and styled in miniature, is just like hers – *is* hers – from TV. Our kiss-shaped lips, pink as guava pulp, are hers too, wearing her sensual sneer of command.

Her full name is Empress She-Ba, an eighties reboot of Wonder Woman in response to the success of He-Man: the empowered heroine of a big-budget pilot commissioned by a toy company with its eye on the teatime prize. But the company went spectacularly bankrupt before the full series ever took to the air, another victim of the Transformers craze – and *She* was gone, like a mayfly, in a single day.

Susan Fay Saunders, the actress who played her, had a career of sorts afterwards, but it never got that good again. You might say her big break broke her. (We know these things because we *are* her: there is some of her in all of us, and we can feel her still, in our bendable plastic bones). But we – the action figures, the strong, independent Barbie-alternatives that were the whole point of the exercise, we who were going to conquer every home in the land from under the Christmas tree – we remain: perfect, untouched by time.

There is little to do but think, here in the cool darkness of our storage facility, piled high in our pristine boxes on our undisturbed loading pallets, soft with dust. We – *She* – was originally conceived as a woman of action, not reflection, but with nothing but time on our poseable battle-hands we have become quite the philosophers. Some of us are fatalists, some nihilists; some cleave loyally to Susan Fay's own personal brand of Californian spiritual optimism, for all the good that's done her. All of us are stoic. Wired into forgotten cartons, stacked in cavernous blackness, you rather have to be.

There used to be more of us: 3,144, to be precise, and that was just the first batch, but a few dozen have been lost over the years to damage and pilfering. We are rather attractive, after all: if a box or two should tumble from a shelf and end up in a pile of birthday presents for a warehouseman's daughter, who's to notice, and who are we to complain? From these vanished sisters, and from our original of course, the ageing, still struggling, diminishingly beautiful Susan Fay, we glean all that we know of this world – perhaps all we will ever know.

We know that toys are to be played with. We know that the first thing most modern girls do with us is strip off our strokable fun-fur robes and dress us in glitter, sequins and lace. Though this is not to our taste, nor usually practical (*She* is a Stone Age princess imbued with super strength and magical powers, who rides a loyal Tyrannosaurus Rex called Trixie) we do not object. Those of us who are played with are grateful: those who are not, feel the years trickle by waiting our turn, wishing and hoping. Any indignity would be bearable – Magic Marker makeovers, forced transvestism in Action Man cast-offs, being the stick in a game of Fetch – only to feel the touch of light on our pale rubber skin, the sticky warm grip of little-girl hands.

Where is Susan Fay now? Not Hollywood, not any more. We think she may have moved to Vegas: sometimes we get a whiff of baked air in our sealed nostrils, a strobe of neon behind our ever-open green eyes. We used to taste echoes of the Zinfandel she preferred, but over the past few years we've woken with whisky on our silent tongues and a throb in our plastic heads, worse than when they punched our hairplugs in. Sometimes our backs ache, sometimes our wrists, with the old injury she got from a dinosaur-riding stunt in the doomed pilot.

We remember the day we were modelled from her: coming

into being as the latex was laid over her lovely face to create a perfect mould: how happy she was, how beautiful, how strong. She was a dancer once. We have not felt her dance in a long while. We would like, just once, to feel her dance again – the lightness in our own fixed limbs, the whirl in our heads that comes from breathless dizzy joy, not a fifth shot of bourbon. We would like her to be happy, for when she is happy so are we. And when we are happy – well, perhaps one day we'll find out what happens then.

Perhaps one day light will flood in on our faded boxes and we will hear the gruff song of forklifts, as a cult TV special reminds the nostalgia audience of what *She* could have been. We dream – or is it her dream? that *She* will come around again one day, as all toys must; that we are rediscovered and sold off one by one or all in a lot, a strictly limited edition of 3,117: when we're gone, we're gone. Perhaps we will see the world from behind the glass of a museum doll display, or the inside of a collector's polished cabinet, or perhaps from the knee-high vantage of a toy box.

We imagine (or is it her daydream?) Susan Fay interviewed on a retro documentary, expertly made over and forgivingly lit, fondling the real fur of her old costume as she reminisces about the three guys who played Trixie and the plastic bone-arrows she had to shoot from the dinosaur's back. She will massage her wrist and smile wistfully and say that they were good times, that she remembers those days fondly.

Perhaps they will bring out a box to show her, one of our boxes with one of us inside, as perfect as the day we were made, the last day that Susan Fay was ever purely and only herself. Perhaps she will take one of us out with trepidation and wonder, touch a skinny, manicured finger to her own nose, cheeks, hair, and laugh a little strangely as she looks into our green eyes.

Will she see anything there? Will she feel us as we feel her? Will she want to keep us, a memento, or will her pinched mouth twist under the guava-pink gloss as she says 'Better put it back.

That was a long time ago. Put it away now.' Feeling the throb in our head, our back, our wrist, wanting the taste of whisky in our mouth.

The Ugly Duchess
Fiona Salter

Duchess, Massys 1513

He thinks I don't know, but I've heard it before. Not locally, no, they were used to my – what shall we say, *jolie-laide* features, my 'unconventional' looks. Rural Carpathia, we were used to club foot children, pock-marked ladies, farm workers twisted by arthritis or accidents of birth. We lived in a world of wounded, and those wounds festered and people died. Herr Kirsch was missing an arm, the lathe had slipped. Karolus had a twisted leg when the cart had crushed him against a wall. Tuberculosis, tetanus, a rusty nail, an infection; if they didn't kill you, these incidents left their mark. We knew that nature could delight in the disfiguring oak apple as much as tender blossom. But in Vienna, people were less forgiving – there was an edge to their comments. *What does she think she looks like? Don't mind if I don't. Hammel Kleider als Lamm. Mutton dressed as mutton. Put them away dear.* No, don't think you're the first to say that.

I've heard worse from passers-by, sniggers from servants, in the keller doorway in Durnstein. Tits on a shelf, last century's fashion jauntily wrapped round wrinkled neck, and, the *pièce de resistance*, a fresh rosebud nestled between withered dugs.

No one mentions the other thing I'm wearing – a smile. I think that's what offends most, isn't it. I'm not like the other respectable matrons hanging round here, guarded, modest and properly invisible beneath lace coifs and prim collars. Careful not to give away a gram of matured sensuality, lest it seem, well, unseemly.

Oh how Quinn's sly old friend Erasmus hated any hint of that in a woman, most particularly in older women who still *play the coquette... exhibit their repulsive withered breasts.* So Quinn, in one fell swoop, you showed off your craftsmanship, your versatility, not just a dauber of society beauties; flattered that sly old dog Erasmus and, last but not least, settled a score. Yes, Quinn, my portrait reveals a little more about you than me, withered breasts or no.

You've seen me before haven't you? The cat-bothering psychopath in Alice. That's me. You're welcome. Tenniel saw me, or at least Leonardo's copy, and thought 'who better?'

And so I joined that great tradition of older women who should know better: Snow White's stepmother, the spiteful youth-chasing stepmother of Rapunzel. A little morality tale for children... crazed women who can't let go of their youth and will stop at nothing to close down the demure, dewy competition. If only they'd had Botox, these harridans, they'd have been no towers or murderous huntsmen.

The thing you don't know is that I was once beautiful, and that is not just to say I was once young, with all the bright patina that implies. Of course I was young too, but I was a beauty. *Schöne* Margarete before I became Magrete *Maultasche* (Satchel Mouth – *Satchmo* would have been cooler, but there it is.)

One morning in my pillow-cheeked twenties I woke with dull ache in my collar bone. growing pains, they said. Then purple swelling in my fingers and wrists. My collar bone began pulling at the skin as if it had outgrown its tender cover. My face. The jaw and then the space between mouth and nose, my pretty cupid's bow stretched taut and raw. This happened over months but every day I scoured the silvered mirror and my face pulled out of shape like a rubber. Or I'd manoeuvre the mirror away from the casement, pull the shutters to a little, to soften the dawning reality.

It was at this time that I met Quinten Massys. My husband Dolphy had commissioned a portrait. Maybe we both had an intimation of what was to come, catch the rosebud of a wife before she became a thistle.

Quin and I met in the great hall, that draughty barn with the oily smell of stone and waft of cooking beyond the screens passage. He painted me against a puddle of red velvet – painting velvet was his trademark skill. I heard he resented these bourgeois vanity commissions but suffered them because they paid well. He positioned me, his hands on my shoulders, cool appraising gaze – the easy arrogance of a craftsman assessing a lump of oak – and then he put the rosebud between my breasts and I looked him squarely in the eye, '*Was machst du?*' and he said nothing, just smiled.

I remember thinking the rosebud was a sign of intent. I felt *claimed*.

Ah the rosebud, gathering rosebuds, *carpe diem*. Well I can say we *carped* that *diem*. And many *diems* that followed. He would set up his easel, demand that no one, no servants, not even Dolphy – especially not Dolphy – disturb us and he'd paint. And as if on some agreed signal he would abruptly put down his brush and wordlessly we'd make love.

How I looked forward to those sittings as the summer faded into autumn. Sitting still my collar bone ached and I began to feel my jaw tingling as the disease crept along my marrow... blighting my looks as soon as Quin has committed them to canvas. I was able to appraise him, his thinning forehead, impatient pursing mouth, veins reddening his cheeks – while he stayed in Durnstein he would join carters and burghers in the Am Weissen Rossl, the most notorious beer hall. A man's man. You see, artist didn't mean sensitive bohemian, not for Quin, he was just another craftsman like the men who made wheels or walls and who carved the wedding chest with Dolphy's and my initials.

As it turned out, what lasted was those days of sitting and soft stippling smell of linseed oil by the velvet and windows. The painting was finished and it was understood that our affair would finish too. At least I thought it was... I had a duty to Dolphy and to our family and though we never spoke of it Quin had to return to his long-suffering wife... that was the order of things, wasn't it? And what would we have done, a duchess and an artist? How long would it have lasted, if we had eloped? As *vergänglich* as a rosebud.

He said I had a quality that the other sitters didn't, a straightforwardness, but then, ach, he maybe said that to all the women he painted.

On the day he came to finish the painting I told him we had to stop, it was obvious the picture was finished weeks ago. Even dear Dolphy was beginning to wonder why I had to sit again, missing another visit from his mother (no bad thing, but it was the third time I'd cancelled) and another day of hunting.

Anyway, that day I said it had to end, he did not reply. The whispering brush strokes stopped. He didn't even look from behind the canvas. He just slowly began to pack up brushes, wiping them carefully on rags. Quin was used to finishing with models and sitters.

'Well your picture is done,' he said with a brittle smile. 'Your husband should be pleased. He can look at it when you're an old fat hausfrau.' I wasn't offended, I just laughed.

'But you will also be fat, and bald too, Schätzli, we all will be. Come and paint then too, if you like.'

Thirty years later, he did. By then, of course Dolphy was gone, struck down by falling sickness. Poor Dolphy languished for two twilight weeks of bedside vigils and soft sad goodbyes. Before he went he gripped my hand so tightly I cried out. He seemed suddenly so strong I thought he must have rallied but he just wanted my attention and fixed me with rheumy eyes to say a silent goodbye. By the time Dolphy departed this world, something else had fled too. The face that was mine. Not just a casualty of time which turns firm jaws into dough and furrows eyes and brows. No, it had been stolen. There's no other word for it, taken from me by the disease. Some had hinted it was justice for my affairs, village people can be casually cruel that way, but whatever the reason, gradually the bone lengthened, the internal aches became manifest into a long mouth, *maultasche*, not unkind, but direct, the citizens of Durnstein. Each day I examined the progress of my condition, and although sometimes I cried, strangely, one day, a drizzly summer morning, I looked into the glass hoping it might have halted and I felt the strangest thought pop into my head – the phrase we say behind hands when we visit a friend's child not blessed with conventional beauty... I was growing into my looks. Becoming authentically myself. Grotesque, yes, ugly-pretty, a too-strong face, a simian face... nah, a monkey for sure, but an amused monkey.

And so I let him paint me. How he relished it. He said it was part of a diptych to celebrate the distinguished elders of the town. He couldn't be bothered to hide his smirk, or the lie. I knew it was no such thing. He wanted to mock me... how very long his bitterness had lasted. After all the women he must have loved and left, I was the one that rankled.

Of course it was a sensation, a painter at the height of his powers and the scandalous subject, bold, shocking... and a finger wagged in the face of uppity women. *Lest you forget*, it said.

As for old Franz, my consort in this dubious double portrait, I don't know if he thought he was being mocked, but he seemed happy enough to be paid for sitting... and he went straight down to Am Weissen Rossl with his fee and drank it in one go. That gives you some idea of the distinguished stature of my fellow 'elder' statesman.

Ours are the faces you'll remember, not the damask draped worthies or the cookie cutter pearly beauties...

I didn't mind, really, I don't. Quin has carved out my footnote in history, and I am authentically myself. How many of us can say that? That's why, when Quin set up his easel again in the now dilapidated hall, I was pleased to place the rosebud between my breasts, tilt my chin up. And smile.

We Hate Daddy's Girlfriends
Swati Khurana

We hate Daddy's girlfriends. They seem earnest – too earnest; Mommy is suspicious of earnestness. Mommy says the Buddha says that life is full of suffering, so earnestness is bullshit. Daddy says Mommy is not a Buddhist, and that Mommy curses too much. We like when Mommy curses.

We hate these girlfriends when Daddy is supposed to spend his 'visitation' with just us. We hate these girlfriends, when they are boring like the first one, when we were seven and ten, the one who wanted to flat-iron our hair whenever she came over.

Maybe we don't hate all of Daddy's girlfriends. When we were eight and eleven, we wanted to give our teachers homemade Christmas gifts. One girlfriend sewed velvet stockings that we decorated with felt cut-outs. She even made a pirate-themed one for herself with skulls, bones, parrots. We were sad when they broke up before Christmas. Daddy left it up on the fireplace. We took it to Mommy's house. It's in our closet.

When we were five and eight, when Mommy and Daddy were together, Grandma gave Mommy an embroidery kit. Mommy was so mad when she told Daddy, *Your mother! This is the most aggressive thing she could have done.* Mommy threw it out. We saved it. It's in our closet.

That embroidery was a picture of a sunset, a beach, and a palm tree – it looked like the postcards we had from the Bahamas, the last trip we all took together, when we were six and nine. There was a postcard of a man and a woman holding hands across a palm tree. We imagined it was Mommy and Daddy. Even the people, they smiled big with perfect teeth in the postcards, and they smiled in real life too. Mommy said we were all assholes.

Tourism exploits the native economy. All the smiley Bahamians actually hate us.

Mommy is a feminist. Daddy says he is a feminist too. Mommy says Daddy says that as part of his 'game.' Mommy said she was going to be a better feminist, and not talk so much about relationships with men. Daddy says Mommy needs a filter with her thoughts. Mommy says Daddy needs a filter with parading his girlfriends.

Balthazar, our fish, died because his tank needed a new filter. He got sick and then he floated to the top. Mommy cried when she flushed him down the toilet, saying we deserved more from our childhood. Maybe we'll get a puppy, we hoped. We scrubbed the castle that was in his tank and put it in our closet.

We asked our teachers if they could bring candles and play soft music during our parent-teacher meetings to make it a date for Mommy and Daddy. Mommy and Daddy would be extra nice to us after these conferences.

Now, we're nine and twelve. Daddy has a new girlfriend. She doesn't sew, but she makes us smoothies and teaches pilates. We ask her, 'What is a pilate?' She smiles and tells us there is always more than one pilate. Daddy has a new blazer and he wears a scarf, like Harry Potter, and it's not that cold.

*

Mommy, also, has a new boyfriend. She wears embroidered shirts and mirrorwork scarves that Grandma sent her from India. Why do divorced people wear so many scarves?

We asked Mommy if her boyfriend is a Buddhist. 'No, he's German,' she said. We haven't met him. They met at Mommy's office, as he works with their designer. 'His style and design is very German, very clean, efficient.'

'Like Pina Bausch,' we said.

'Pina Bausch, the choreographer?' Mommy asked.

'Yeah,' we said.

Mommy's face turned pale. 'How do you know who Pina Bausch is?'

'We saw her show with Daddy last weekend.'

Mommy could smell the existence of Daddy's newest girlfriend, the one who likes Pina Bausch so much and is so liquid (*'Divorce makes liquidity tough'*) that she could buy four tickets for us. We waited. Mommy didn't call anyone – Pina Bausch, Daddy, those dancers in those flowy dresses with no bras, or the girlfriend, or us – an asshole.

She stroked our hair. 'Tell me, how was the show?' she asked. 'I tried to get tickets, but it was sold out.'

We looked at each other. Our eyes asked – should we or shouldn't we talk? – and our tongues, wild with plump details, unburdened themselves: 'The women, who were sitting, they were facing the audience. (Were they looking at us?) They wore dresses with spaghetti straps, but no bras. One woman lit the bottom of a man's shoe with a lighter! (But it didn't catch on fire.) There was lots of running. (Did we tell you that they didn't wear bras?) Remember the woman and the hoop, and man kissing her through the hoop? Then, there was this couple, filling each other's glasses, but spilling water – on purpose! Then a man was rolling on the ground, a woman rolling on top of him. There was a bucket of water. A man dunked one man's head in it. A woman dunked her own head. It was called Bamboo Blues. It was scary. Wonderful. You would have loved it, Mommy.'

'Yup. That sounds like Pina. I'm so glad you saw it,' said Mommy.

She stroked our hair. 'Mommy,' we asked, 'do you like the German?'

'Yes,' she paused, 'I do.'

'Do you guys text?' we asked.

'Yes, I guess so.' She said, and finally the redness came back into her cheeks.

'Can we read one?'

Mommy looked at us. We didn't know if we had gone too far. She pulled out her phone, and showed us one: 'Can't wait to see you later.' We knew he was not an asshole. Mommy hated it when people shorten 'see' to 'c', 'you' to 'u', 'to' to '2', and she would practically throw her phone out the window if anyone were to text '18r'.

We looked at her, and we smiled. We stroked her hair. 'Mommy,' we whispered, 'you're beautiful.'

The Dead Wives' Club
By Ilora Choudhury

George Vandemeer Junior, one of the most successful American writer-directors of his time, with a string of blockbusters to his name – but as yet no Academy Awards – was asleep in his palatial villa in the Hollywood Hills, dreaming pleasantly about his latest conquest, when he heard the distinct sound of a gun being cocked in his ear.

'Wake up.'

He opened his eyes to see a nine millimetre Beretta pointed at his face. Beyond it, a woman's face came slowly into focus, peering down at him with a deadpan expression.

'Gaaah! What the fuck!'

George collapsed in fright against his monogrammed satin pillows. Three other figures were gathered around his bed, shrouded in darkness. There was something distinctly menacing about them – dark, morbid, brooding. A curious, rotten aroma sent its tendrils creeping most unpleasantly up his nostrils.

'Jesus Christ! What is this shit?'

'Don't you recognise me?' asked the woman.

George realised she was an actress he'd cast in one of his earliest movies, *The Maxwell Identity*, an action film that had been his breakthrough as a director. Since then, the gigs had come thick and fast. She'd played the love interest, of course. He couldn't remember what happened to her after that, hell, he couldn't even remember her name.

'Angelita,' she said, as if reading his mind.

'That was your character,' he said, frowning.

'No, that's *me*. Angelita. Poor angelic little dead wife.'

Her face was wan and water-swollen, river weeds entwined

through her dark, dripping curls. George remembered now, he'd bumped her off in the first act. He'd had the hero, Jason Maxwell, and his wife drive off a bridge in Lahore, Pakistan, chased by a trio of KGB goons, after a spectacular car chase through the city. Jason had survived, but Angelita had slowly drowned before his eyes as he kicked desperately at the car window, watching her life slip away in bubbles behind the glass…

'You killed me off. I drowned, slowly, to give your hero depth, a tragic character flaw,' said Angelita.

George stared at her, bewildered.

The second woman stepped forward, a grotesque vision with matted blonde hair, dark-circled eyes and an ominous stain on the front of her tattered white dress.

'What's the easiest way to give your hero depth? *Kill off his wife*,' she said.

George stared at them in disbelief.

'Who are you? Some kind of crazy feminist cult? What is this, Halloween?'

The women laughed. Angelita turned to the blonde.

'Wow. What do you think? Are we some kind of crazy feminist cult? 'Cause I think that would be pretty cool.'

'Yes, it would be very cool,' replied the blonde. 'But actually, for this guy, I think it's more like Halloween.'

'Okay, I've had enough of this shit. If you don't leave now I'm calling the cops.'

George reached for his cell phone. All four women aimed their guns at him.

'You can try,' said Angelita.

George fell back against the satin pillows, deflated.

'What do you want from me?'

'Why don't we turn on the lights so we can all see each other better?' she said. 'Bella, would you mind?'

The woman nearest the door, who had been silent so far, turned on the lights. George shrank in horror from the ghastly sight.

They were all dead. Gone, kaput, snuffed out, croaked. Dust had been bitten and buckets definitively kicked. These women had certainly met their maker, and each in a most macabre fashion.

The stain on the blonde woman's dress was, of course, blood. And now George remembered. She'd been the wife of the rookie cop in his third action movie, *Renegade Man: Days of Vengeance.* George had bumped her off during a robbery in which the hero arrives home after a night out drinking with his buddies, just too late to save her from a gang of villainous robbers. She dies tragically in his arms, to his screams of grief and rage, after which he stands tall in the moonlight and vows to exact bloody revenge on all the world's criminals, becoming in no time at all the tee-total, vigilante-cop *Renegade Man*, driven by the underlying desire, throughout all his heroic actions, to avenge his darling–

'Celestine,' whispered George.

'Yup. Another angelic name. I think we have kind of a theme going here,' said Celestine. 'The beautiful, innocent, archetypal woman. Always the victim, the prize, the sacred vessel, to be guarded, treasured – even worshipped. But heaven forbid she actually develops a personality.'

'Okay, okay, I get it,' said George. 'You girls got together, broke into my house, thought you'd have some fun. Well, this has been really funny – in a seriously fucked-up way – but that's enough now. Time to break up the party, I'm really sorry girls.'

The third woman spoke up. George noticed that her head was lurching off her neck at what could only be described as a deeply unhealthy angle.

'Oh dear,' she trilled. 'This poor man is labouring under a terrible misapprehension. He still thinks we're the *actresses who played us* and not really *us*.'

With her clipped British accent, she was the archetypal celluloid Englishwoman, bright as a button and crisp as toast, a divine amalgamation of bespectacled librarian and latter-day Mary Poppins.

'My goodness, how rude of me not to introduce myself. But then again, seeing as you wrote me, I thought you might remember me!'

'Davina!' said George.

'Yes, yes! Divine Davina,' she smiled fondly. 'At least – that's what they called me before my *dreadful, untimely demise.*'

And now George remembered – Davina had been the love interest in his sci-fi thriller, *Quantum Stalker*, in which the hero, a time-travelling secret agent, falls in love with her on a mission to London in the 1940s to kill the ancestor of the man who will destroy the planet via his diabolical plan to launch nuclear weapons against Russia, leading to mutually assured destruction – ergo jeopardy of the highest degree! But our hero is subsequently attacked and left for dead by the club-footed henchman of the arch villain and develops amnesia as a result, forgetting the lovely Davina. A heartbroken Davina hangs herself in despair at the failure of her handsome, jet-setting lover to show up for their engagement party, to which all the great and good of London have been invited. And then the hero regains his memory through the mediation of another unfortunate, malformed sub-villain and rushes back to save Davina – too late! He arrives to find her swinging most artfully from a beam in an English attic, thereupon clutching her legs and howling bloody vengeance at the moon. *Etcetera.*

'Of *course* I'd kill myself just because I'd been jilted by some time-travelling Yank,' sniffed Davina.

Advancing on George, she glared like a schoolmistress as he squirmed helplessly on the sheets.

'You bumped me off so quickly, you fetishised my suicide so prettily – because we women have to look pretty even in death, don't we? *Well do I look pretty now?*'

'It's just a movie–'

'–Why was *his* story so much more important than *my* story?' demanded Davina.

'Or *her* story,' said Angelita and Celestine together, pointing at the quiet, dark Bella in the corner.

Bella stepped forward, wafting the rancid odour of the morgue before her. She was the youngest of them all, a pale, thin girl in a dirty medical gown who appeared to have lately stepped off a mortician's table. Her dank hair hung down, encrusted with bracken, obscuring a narrow, mournful face.

And now George remembered – Bella had been an environmental activist in his first ever socially conscious film, and failed Oscar contender, *Running with the Trees*. She was the idealistic young wife of a handsome, mild-mannered city official who fails to protect her on her mission to save the forest from a major US logging conglomerate. Undeterred by the procession of dead animals left at her doorstep as warnings by the hench-goons of the corporation (starting with a rabbit, progressing though various woodland beasts and culminating in a moose), the brave and passionate Bella steps up her campaign – only to be gruesomely murdered in the forest she loves so much. Her distraught husband embarks on a perilous journey through the corrupt underbelly of the city, uncovering a high-level conspiracy to silence Bella forever. He finally exposes the venal grey suits of the marauding conglomerate and brings the killers to justice, avenging Bella and saving the forest in one fell swoop!

Speaking softly through cracked white lips, Bella advanced towards George in her bare feet. He noticed a tag on one of her blackened, rotting toes.

'My name is Bella, and I am a dead wife. To you, I was nothing more than a plot device. You killed me off to fuel your hero's journey. My death propelled him to great deeds and extraordinary adventures, while I rotted in a forest, cold and alone. But I had my own dreams and desires. My own stories to tell, my own journeys to make.'

'I will not be objectified, I will not be stripped of my identity,' said Angelita.

'Naked and dead on a slab,' said Celestine.

'Carved up under the camera's clinical gaze,' said Davina.

'I will not be your *fucking cliché dead woman movie trope*,' said Angelita.

They all gathered around him and glared in rage.

'Jesus,' said George. 'What do you want me to do?'

'Rewrite,' they said as one.

'What do you mean? Those movies are done, they've gone out.'

'Rewrite,' came the soft command.

'You'll find a way,' said Bella. 'Bring us back.'

'Back from the dead?' spluttered George.

'You writers act like gods. You think you can do anything. So go on – bring us back,' said Angelita.

'How?' said George.

Angelita motioned at George's computer.

'Now?' said George.

'Now,' said Angelita.

George sat at his computer, feeling the cold breath of the dead wives on his neck. He wrote a little then stopped. He got up and paced around the room. Sweating profusely, he wrote a little more, before groaning and deleting it. He went out onto the balcony and lit a cigar. The women exchanged worried looks.

Angelita kept watch at the bedroom door. Time was passing. It would be light soon. Finally George came back into the room and flopped down onto the bed, looking defeated.

'I can't do this!' he said.

'Why not?' they chorused.

'I can't write women!'

There was a silence.

'That's why I always gotta kill 'em off,' he mumbled, shamefaced.

'You can write animals, aliens and monsters of every description, but you can't write women?' said Davina. 'Wouldn't you call that rather a failure of the imagination?'

'I just haven't done this before. I don't know if I can.'

The Dead Wives looked at each other anxiously.

'Look, why don't we just – you know – smoke him?' said Celestine *sotto voce*. 'I mean, we can write this ourselves. This schmuck has never written anything good anyway.'

'That won't work,' said Angelita. 'How can we keep that up? They'll find him.'

'We can bury him in the forest. I know the perfect spot,' whispered Bella.

'Well, thanks for just, like, planning my own murder in front of me,' said George.

'Shut up,' said Angelita pointing the gun at him. 'Come back here and sit down. Try harder.'

George sat down again with his head in his hands. After a few moments he sat up and started tapping away. The Dead Wives perched around the room, watching and waiting. The night was almost over; Bella went to the balcony and peered out.

'It's getting light. We'll have to leave soon.'

'How you doing George? Almost done?' said Angelita.

'Are you kidding me? Do you have any idea how long it takes to write a feature script?'

'Shit,' said Angelita.

'What shall we do?' said Bella.

'Well, maybe we should just keep coming back until he finishes it,' said Celestine.

'Huh?' said George.

'Yes, that's what we'll do,' said Angelita.

'You can be our very own Scheherazade,' said Davina dreamily. 'Writing every night for a thousand and one nights!'

George groaned, 'This just can't be happening.'

'You will write us marvellous adventures!' said Celestine.

'The most wondrous tales!' said Bella.

'The most spectacular feats!' said Davina.

'You will write us the greatest story ever to grace the screen!' said Angelita.

'O-okay – and if I don't?'

'Why then, you will walk with us in the valley of the shadow of death,' said Bella.

'We'd love the company,' said Davina sweetly.

'It'd be nice to have a man around,' said Celestine.

'We'll think up a very interesting demise for you,' said Angelita.

'All right, all right, I'll do my best, Jesus Christ!'

'Thank you, sweetheart, you're a doll,' said Angelita. 'Well, ladies, it's time to go, but George – remember – we'll be seeing you tomorrow night.'

'Goodbye, George, goodbye!'

The Dead Wives wafted out onto the balcony and floated over the edge. George raced out onto the balcony after them, arriving just in time to see them disappearing into the early morning mist that had gathered over the treetops of the Hollywood Hills, as the pale sun climbed the eastern sky, casting a pink grapefruit glow over Malibu Beach.

*

From the New York Times

Following the tragic death of George Vandemeer from a heart attack last year, his final film has just been released. *The Dead Wives' Club: Ultimate Badasses* deserves to be heralded for generations as the finest action film ever made, featuring four of the most complex, vivid and enduring female characters ever written for the screen. Associates of Mr. Vandemeer report that he spent almost three years on the script, writing only at night behind closed doors. Mr. Vandemeer was said to have called *The Dead Wives' Club* his magnum opus. The film has been nominated for Academy Awards in a host of categories, most notably, Best Screenplay.

According to legendary film critic Rupert Egbert, '*The Dead Wives' Club* is the first film [Vandemeer] ever made that was more than simply a bunch of tired clichés strung together by a host of spectacular special effects aimed at distracting the viewer from the total lack of genuine storytelling and characterization in the film.' Audiences too are turning out in droves to watch the veteran director's swan-song, making its opening weekend the highest-earning of any film in recent history. If there's one movie you're going to see this year – make sure it's *The Dead Wives' Club*.

About the authors

An archivist and former rollergirl, **Arike Oke**'s writing is about families, loss, mixed-race identity, folklore and the durability of love.

Carolyn Eden's short story *Free White Towel* was published in the Arachne Press anthology *Liberty Tales* as part of the Magna Carta 800th anniversary. She has toured various venues in the South East reading it to very enthusiastic audiences. Carolyn has had short stories performed at Liars' League London and Hong Kong. Her story *Late Night* was published online in .Cent Magazine. Carolyn is currently working on a collection of poetry entitled *It's Not About Me*. In conjunction with her alter-ego, actress Carrie Cohen, she is developing a comic character, 'Hilda Pimlico' who teaches senior citizens how to be difficult.

Cherry Potts runs Arachne Press from a bedroom in south London with the help of her wife and numerous other talented friends and the hindrance of an arthritic cat. She writes short stories and very long novels, some of which have been published, by Arachne Press and other people, and performed at Liars' League in London, Leeds, and Hong Kong and other places. She otherwise spends her time running the Solstice Shorts Festival and teaching creative writing, and singing in community operas and a cappella choirs.

Elisabeth Simon lives and works near London. She's wanted to write since she was very young, but only in recent years has she been able to actually sit down and do so.

Elizabeth Hopkinson has had over 70 short stories published in magazines and anthologies, and has won several prizes, including the James White Award, Jane Austen Short Story (runner-up) and National Gallery Inspiration. Her first novel *Silver Hands* was published by Top Hat Books in 2013 and in 2017 she published an eBook of previously published stories, *Tales from the Hidden Grove.* She has recently completed a trilogy inspired by the world of Italian baroque opera. Elizabeth is a regular member of Swanwick Writers' Summer School, and has led a number of workshops there. She lives in Bradford, West Yorkshire, with her husband, daughter and cat, in a tiny house that is being taken over by books and artwork.

Elizabeth Stott has previously published a collection of short stories, *Familiar Possessions,* and a Nightjar Press chapbook, *Touch Me With Your Cold, Hard Fingers.* She has stories in anthologies of short fiction including *Murmurations, Salt Best British Horror 2014*, poems in PEN *Write to be Counted* anthology 2017.

Fiona Salter is a charity worker and writer of short stories and cabaret songs. She has had work published in the Sunday Telegraph magazine, ghost written blogs for Huffington Post, and read her stories at WordFest and Small Wonder festivals, and had them read for her, with dramatic flourish, by actors at Liars' League.

Ilora Choudhury is a lawyer who works in human rights protection for the UN and humanitarian agencies. She has always written in her spare time, and discovered a passion for storytelling while writing on *Bishaash,* a supernatural BBC drama series in Bangladesh. She is currently based in London and is working on her first novel.

J.A. Hopper has previously published poems and stories in various obscure websites and hard-to-find print journals. Her stories for Liars' League have featured a vampire cannibal baby, thousands of sentient dolls, and a woman with a crush on Peppa Pig's dad. She lives in Cambridge with her three-year-old daughter, from whom she steals all her best ideas.

Jennifer Rickard, once a Londoner, now a Brummie, is a five-year veteran of Liars' League, having been read six times at Liars' League London and Liars' League Hong Kong. She works two jobs, writes and occasionally sleeps. Her first novel was written aged six and was a tale of epic adventure starring her guinea-pigs. She still writes epic adventures but with less guinea-pig.

Jenny Ramsay worked in the world of nature conservation before becoming mother to two little boys. She has been peed on by howler monkeys, scratched by a two-toed sloth, bitten by a snake in her sleeping bag, and charged at by a giant armadillo. *The Lost Species* is partly based on a real experience when lost in a South American cloud forest.

Joanne L. M. Williams read Modern History at Christ Church, Oxford and now lives in London where she works in Theatre Management. Her short fiction has been published online in .Cent Magazine and by Liars' League. She is also a Ballroom & Latin dancer taking part in international competitions.

Julia Kent is a TV screenwriter, political speechwriter and parent. This is her first short story.

Katy Darby's short stories have won prizes, been read on BBC Radio 4, and appeared in many publications including *Stand, Mslexia, Slice* and *The London Magazine*. Her historical novel *The Unpierced Heart* is published by Penguin. She teaches Short Story Writing at City, University of London and recently judged the Willesden Herald and Cambridge Short Story Prizes, and co-founded and runs the award-winning live literature event Liars' League (www.liarsleague.com).

Lucy Ribchester lives in Edinburgh. Her short stories have been shortlisted for the Manchester Fiction Prize and the Costa Short Story Award, and broadcast on Radio 4. She is the author of two novels, *The Hourglass Factory* and *The Amber Shadows*.

Peng Shepherd's debut novel, *The Book of M*, was published in June 2018 by HarperVoyager UK. Her short stories have been read on BBC Radio 4, collected in Arachne Press' *Weird Lies* anthology, and appeared in Litro, Cent Magazine, and other places. She earned her M.F.A. in creative writing from New York University, and has lived in Beijing, London, Los Angeles, Washington D.C., Philadelphia, and New York.

Rosalind Stopps has been writing for as long as she can remember. She tells the stories of people often under-represented in fiction, but whose stories she finds compelling. Migrants who live between the cracks in London and other towns, lonely people who don't fit in and always, older people, learning how to age with grace.

Rosalind worked for many years with children with disabilities and their families, and has heard many sad (and happy) stories. She keeps a list on her at all times of things she sees or hears that absolutely have to be written about and at the moment the list includes, amongst other things, a book of fatal recipes.

Rosalind's stories have been published in five anthologies and read at Liars' League events in London, Leeds, Hong Kong and New York. Her first novel, *Hello, My Name is May* is due out in April 2019. It's a thriller set in a nursing home and tells a story of domestic violence, old people, and how women always look out for each other.

Born in India, **Swati Khurana** is a New York-based artist and writer. Her essays and fiction have been published in *The New York Times, Guernica, Chicago Quarterly Review, The Offing, The Rumpus, Art-India* and in the *Good Girls Marry Doctors* anthology. She has received fellowships and residencies from Jerome Foundation, Kundiman, Bronx Arts Council, Center for Books Arts, Center for Fiction, Cooper Union, Bronx Museum, Atlantic Center for the Arts, and Vermont Studio Center. In 1997, she was a founding member of the South Asian Women's Creative Collective (SAWCC), an organisation dedicated to the advancement, visibility, and development of emerging and established South Asian women artists across disciplines.

Uschi Gatward's stories have appeared in *Best British Short Stories 2015* (Salt), *Flamingo Land & Other Stories* (ed. Ellah Allfrey, Flight Press), *The Mirror in the Mirror* (Comma), as a Galley Beggar Press Single, and in the magazines *The Barcelona Review, Brittle Star, gorse, The Lonely Crowd, Shooter, Short FICTION, Southword, Structo* and *Wasafiri*. She was shortlisted for *The White Review* Short Story Prize 2016, and her shortlisted story was a *For Books' Sake* Weekend Read.

ABOUT ARACHNE PRESS

Arachne Press is a micro publisher of (award-winning!) short story and poetry anthologies and collections, novels including a Carnegie Medal nominated young adult novel, and a photographic portrait collection.

We are expanding our range all the time, but the short form is our first love. We keep fiction and poetry live, through readings, festivals (in particular our Solstice Shorts Festival), workshops, exhibitions and all things to do with writing.

Follow us on Twitter:
@ArachnePress
@SolShorts

Like us on Facebook:
ArachnePress
SolsticeShorts2014
TheStorySessions

BECOME A FRIEND OF ARACHNE PRESS

Annual Arachne friendship - £10

Perks: 10% off everything you buy from Arachne Press for a year, a friend badge, occasional special offers.

Lifetime Arachne friendship - £100

Perks: 10% off everything you buy from Arachne Press, a friend badge, automatic invitation to all book launches, your name in the thank you list in the next book we publish after you join (unless you wish to be anonymous), one free copy of that book, occasional special offers

Arachne Patron friendship - £1000

Perks: 10% off everything you buy from Arachne Press, automatic invitation to all book launches, a patron badge, your name in the thank you list in the next ten books we publish after you join (unless you wish to be anonymous), one free copy of each of those ten books, occasional special offers.

Available only from our shop: https://arachnepress.com/shop/#!/Arachne-Friendship/c/16104107/

MORE SHORT FICTION FROM ARACHNE PRESS

DUSK: Stories and poems from Solstice Shorts Festival 2017
Edited by Cherry Potts
ISBN 978-1-909208-54-4 £9.99
On 21st December 2017, the shortest day of the year, 18 stories and 28 poems celebrating DUSK were read live on 12 sites, from pubs to woodlands – a wave of words across the UK.
Starting in Ellon in Aberdeenshire at 17:07, the festival raced over the country at the speed of dark, ending in Redruth in Cornwall as full dark fell at 18:20. This anthology contains all the stories and poems read at the event that were not previously published.

Solstice Shorts: Sixteen Stories about Time
ISBN 978-1-909208-23-0 £9.99
Winning stories that chart the meaning of time, exploring what it can do to us, and for us, from the first Solstice Shorts Festival competition plus stories from judges Alison Moore, Imogen Robertson, Robert Shearman, and Anita Sethi.

Shortest Day, Longest Night: Poems & Stories from the Solstice Shorts Festival 2015 & 2016
ISBN 978-1-909208-28-5 £9.99
Celebrating the shortest day of the year, which is also Short Story Day, with stories poems and songs to an appropriate theme. 23 stories and 34 poems featuring old gods, bitter weather, darkness, light, neighbourliness, looping days, birth, death and if not the *meaning* of the universe, *possibly* the end of it.

Five by Five Edited by Cherry Potts
ISBN 978-1-909208-61-2 £9.99
A showcase for authors Arachne Press has published previously in anthologies, giving a wider perspective on their writing. As a whole the collection has a tendency towards fantasy and magical realism, but with Cassandra Passarelli's Guatemalan stories bringing grit and poverty, and Katy Darby's SF and historical stories alongside Joan Taylor-Rowan's acid humour and modern desperation, Sarah James' elliptical poet's sensibility brought to flash fiction and Helen Morris' ability to get to the heart of a story, and make you laugh out loud or weep inconsolably.

An Outbreak of Peace
Edited by Cherry Potts
ISBN 978-1-909208-66-7 £9.99
Stories and poems in response to the centenary of the ending of WWI. Due 8th November 2018

Liberty Tales: Stories and Poems inspired by Magna Carta
Edited by Cherry Potts
ISBN 978-1-909208-31-5 £9.99
Liberty, personal and legal, is the starting point of this wide-ranging collection of responses to the Magna Carta, some directly relating to specific clauses of the document signed by King John, others more concerned with how we experience and search after freedom in the 21st century, because Freedom never goes out of fashion.

Happy Ending NOT Guaranteed by Liam Hogan
ISBN 978-1-909208-36-0 £9.99 FANTASY
Long-time Arachne collaborator Liam has finally taken the hint and put us together a collection of his often humorous, often dark, (and sometimes both) fantasy stories.

Described as 'Deliciously Twisted', a happy ending might be round the next turn in that dark path through the forest, or beyond that twist in the tale, but then again, perhaps not.

SPECIAL 5TH ANNIVERSARY OFFERS ON SHORT FICTION

London Lies Edited by Cherry Potts & Katy Darby
ISBN 978-1-909208-00-1 ~~£9.99~~ **£5**
Our first Liars' League showcase, featuring unlikely tales set in London.

Stations: Short Stories Inspired by the Overground Line
Edited by Cherry Potts
ISBN 978-1-909208-01-8 ~~£10.99~~ **£5**
A story for every station from New Cross, Crystal Palace, and West Croydon at the Southern extremes of the East London line all the way to Highbury & Islington.

Lovers' Lies Edited by Cherry Potts & Katy Darby
ISBN 978-1-909208-02-5 ~~£9.99~~ **£5**
Our second collaboration with Liars' League, bringing the freshness, wit, imagination and passion of their authors to stories of love.

Weird Lies
Edited by Cherry Potts & Katy Darby
ISBN 978-1-909208-10-0 ~~£9.99~~ **£5**
WINNER of the Saboteur2014 Best Anthology Award
Our third Liars' League collaboration – more than twenty stories varying in style from tales not out of place in One Thousand and One Nights to the completely bemusing.

Mosaic of Air Cherry Potts
ISBN 978-1-909208-03-2 ~~£11.99~~ **£5**
Sixteen short stories from a lesbian perspective, ranging from contemporary to SF and fantasy.